Brief encounter

"I can hardly say it's a pleasure to see *you* again," Grace murmured wryly, giving him a rueful smile that was as composed as her words, feeling a small tug of satisfaction as she saw the slight narrowing of his eyes.

"Oh, but *I* wasn't embarrassed at all...." Scott Gregory's voice was as smooth and controlled as her own, but it contained a stingingly provocative amusement that was like a slap on the face.

" —and we weren't actually introduced," she continued evenly, as if he hadn't interrupted, clinging grimly to her poise.

"In fact, you *could* say that you only provided the bare essentials...."

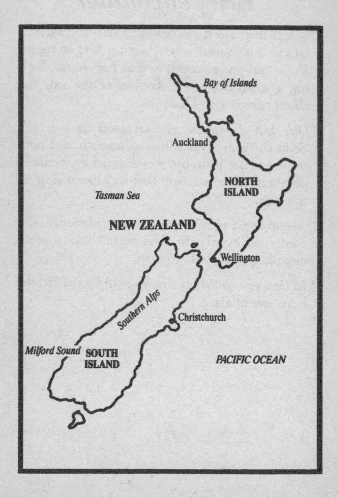

Bay of Islands

Auckland

**NORTH
ISLAND**

Tasman Sea

NEW ZEALAND

Wellington

Southern Alps

Christchurch

Milford Sound **SOUTH
ISLAND**

PACIFIC OCEAN

SUSAN NAPIER

Secret Admirer

Harlequin Books

TORONTO • NEW YORK • LONDON
AMSTERDAM • PARIS • SYDNEY • HAMBURG
STOCKHOLM • ATHENS • TOKYO • MILAN
MADRID • WARSAW • BUDAPEST • AUCKLAND

Harlequin Presents first edition May 1993
ISBN 0-373-11554-7

Original hardcover edition published in 1992
by Mills & Boon Limited

SECRET ADMIRER

CHAPTER ONE

As soon as the lift doors slid open Grace darted inside and reached out to stab at the control panel. Only then did she see the two people standing against the side wall. Her hand froze and the heart that had been pounding fit to burst took off on another fit of frenzy. She took an infinitesimal step backwards towards the already closing doors, her fingers clutching at the collar of her full-length coat. The doors jerked to a stop and began to slide open again.

The man raised a bored black eyebrow. 'Changed your mind?' It was a voice wearied by cynicism, bespeaking a man used to the eternal vacillations of the weaker sex. Grace ignored him, her panicked brain mentally measuring the distance to the emergency stairwell.

She heard the distant sound of a door opening and rapid footsteps muffled on the thick carpet of the hallway. The momentary hesitation had sealed her fate. She would never make the stairwell now. She stepped hurriedly into the depths of the lift, hitting buttons at random and flattening herself up against the opposite wall.

To her relief it immediately began to descend smoothly, retreating from the threat of the eighteenth floor. She couldn't relax, however. The couple standing opposite obviously hadn't heard of the polite rule that required strangers in lifts to avoid looking directly at the other occupants. Grace's hand tightened on her collar. She drew on all her old training to withstand their open gaze—one of envy on the woman's part, cool uninterest on the man's. Already perspiring from her dash to freedom, Grace could feel fresh beads of sweat break out on her skin. Nervously she smoothed the thick black fur over her hips with her free hand.

The woman's exquisitely made-up eyes followed the movement. She was small and fragile, the kind of woman who always made Grace feel a twinge of the teenage angst she had endured when she had suddenly shot to her full height of five foot eleven while all her friends remained blissfully shorter than their boyfriends. She had been taught to regard her height as an advantage rather than a flaw but there were still times that she wished she were small enough to hide in a crowd . . . or a semi-empty lift. Was it her panicked imagination or were they moving only very slowly? She had thought that all these new high-tech skyscrapers had the latest in high-speed technology. Of course, appearances could be very deceptive, as she had just discovered to her cost . . .

Grace stared hard at the blinking light which signalled the slow passing of the floors, willing it to speed up. Out of the corner of her eye she could see the man staring at her lifted profile. Was he looking at her nose? 'Strong' was the euphemism that people tossed around but Grace knew what she saw in the mirror every morning. Her nose was too big for the perfect oval of her face, too distinctive. Like her height, another 'advantage' that she had been encouraged to flaunt rather than conceal. She knew without vanity that she was beautiful, but not in the classical sense of the word. Her features taken piece by piece were far from perfect—apart from her nose, her blue eyes were too widely spaced, her mouth too full—but together with her gleaming cap of midnight-black hair they formed a striking whole. Her beauty was 'unique' and in this era of mass-production uniqueness had an inflationary value.

She had a good mind to turn her head and stare rudely back at *his* flaws, but she didn't want to provoke any confrontation, even a fleeting, silent one. He was tall, taller even than Grace in her two-inch heels, and dark, the perfect foil for the petite redhead beside him, but that was all Grace's brief, horrified first glance had allowed her to take in.

Come on! Her mental urgings became desperate. At this rate Steve was going to have time to be in the foyer before them and she shuddered to think what sort of confrontation that would provoke.

'Is that real animal fur?'

Grace stiffened, little alarm bells jingling within the jangle of her mind. The delicate feminine features opposite were now drawn tight with pouting distaste. Had she mistaken disgust for envy? She gave an inward groan, forcing herself to look politely into the woman's challenging green eyes as she replied in the deep, firm voice that, the elocutionist had taught her, communicated command of one's self and environment.

'Ranch mink.' And worth a small fortune. Grace could see the thought drifting through the woman's mind. No, she hadn't mistaken the envy. But envy didn't necessarily indicate approval.

'A gift?'

The assumption of the question being that a woman could never afford to buy such a luxury out of her own earnings. She needed a rich husband or lover to do that. Oh, how women could unthinkingly perpetuate the injustices of man! Unfortunately, in this case, *especially* in this case, it was the truth.

'Of a sort,' Grace acceded grimly, pulling the coat more closely to her body as she recalled the unpalatable circumstances of her expensive new acquisition.

'Do you think that because animals are farmed for the purpose that makes it all right to kill them simply for the sake of human greed and vanity?'

Grace agreed entirely with the point the other woman was making, but she could hardly say so while swathed in tens of thousands of dollars' worth of black mink. She retreated behind the mental barriers that had served her well in the past.

'I think it's up to individuals to be responsible for their own ethical and moral judgements,' she murmured coolly.

'You don't care what——?'

A sudden jolt interrupted the beginning of what promised to be a full-blooded lecture. Thanking the lord that she could at last escape, Grace waited impatiently for the doors to open. When they didn't she pressed the 'Open Door' button, jiggling it frantically when it failed to respond.

'I don't think that's going to do you any good.'

Again that irritating dry, masculine resignation. Evidently he didn't even believe a woman capable of opening a door!

'Be my guest,' said Grace glacially as she stepped back and released her collar long enough to gesture towards the control panel.

'It's not the door that's stuck,' he said, pressing several of the floor buttons with a strong, olive-skinned hand. 'It's the lift.'

'You mean we're trapped!' The other woman's voice pitched dangerously towards a screech.

Trapped in a lift with a claustrophobic animal-rights campaigner, thought Grace semi-hysterically; that was just what she needed to soothe her overwrought nerves.

The man murmured something soothing as he picked up the emergency telephone. There was an air of authority about him that indicated someone used to taking command. Grace took the opportunity to study him surreptitiously as she absently followed the one-sided conversation.

He was dressed, as was the woman, for an evening out, his dark suit superbly tailored to wide shoulders and lean hips. His olive skin wasn't the result of an unseasonable tan. His black hair, broad high cheekbones and deep-set black eyes hinted at a Latin heritage— Spanish, perhaps, or Italian. His suit and gleaming black shoes were certainly Italian, thought Grace, studying them with a knowledgeable eye. His male chauvinism was probably as much a product of his heritage as of the natural arrogance indicated by the aggressive tilt of his jaw and his clipped manner of speaking. With a little nudge of spite Grace noticed that his own nose was by no means unobtrusive. Definitely a noble Roman nose, although to her chagrin she had to admit that it perfectly balanced those heavy-lidded eyes and finely arched brows.

'It looks as if we may as well get comfortable.' He turned away from the phone, unbuttoning his jacket to reveal a pale grey pleated silk shirt.

'There's something wrong with the lift...? Are we going to crash?' The woman clutched at the side of the lift. Then, thinking better of it, clung to the man's arm instead.

He smiled down at her, but still with that cool edge of detachment that grated on Grace's nerves. 'An electrical fault. Apparently they've been having a few teething problems with the systems in the building, so they're calling the engineer in. I'm assured it won't take long to fix once they arrive, so we shouldn't be more than an hour——'

'An *hour*?' Grace's appalled exclamation overrode his companion's wail that they would miss the show for which they had tickets.

The cold black gaze settled firmly on her flushed face. 'Did you have an urgent...appointment? Do you want to talk to the caretaker? He could no doubt pass on a message for you...'

'No, thank you.' Apart from the fact that there was no one who would miss her for a few hours—or all night, for that matter—Grace found herself loath to move from the comforting solidity of the side of the lift. That would take her closer to the tall, dark stranger; too close. For all his relaxed resignation there was a restless tension about him, a leashed energy that she found threatening. She held her body stiffly, warding off the unreasoning fear.

'Are you claustrophobic?' His voice expressed concern, but there was no warmth or sympathy in the sharp eyes that studied her tension.

Grace shook her head, her slippery black hair briefly fanning out above the lush mink collar. She wrapped her arms around her waist to try to ease the knot in her stomach.

'You might find it a good idea to take off your coat. I'm afraid the air-conditioning in the entire building is out and it may get fairly warm in here.'

Fortunately he was too busy helping the tiny redhead remove her flounced green taffeta evening-coat as he spoke to notice Grace's reaction to his suggestion, and by the time he looked up she had her ragged emotions more or less under control.

'I never feel the heat. I'm very cold-blooded,' she said evenly, thrusting her balled hands into the deep side pockets of the coat as she answered his unspoken enquiry. No doubt he was used to women leaping to obey his every suggestion!

He finished attending to his escort and looked thoughtfully at Grace's defensive attitude for a few agonising moments, before acceding with a quietness that verged on unlikely gentleness, 'As you wish.'

Although he hadn't moved, Grace had the impression of a threat backing off. The fists in her pockets unfurled slightly.

He made a few other quiet, soothing comments, obviously intended to put both women at their ease, but Grace's acute self-awareness was such that she couldn't relax her wary stance enough to respond with anything other than monosyllables. Eventually the couple ignored her completely, conversing in a kind of intimate, low-voiced shorthand that told Grace that they were more than just friends. She also noticed that, while the woman touched the man frequently, smiled and flirted with her eyes and words, he was noticeably restrained. Whatever caused his restraint, Grace felt instinctively that it wasn't her own presence. He didn't much look like a man who cared what others thought of him. He looked like a man who took what he wanted, when he wanted it, on his own terms. There was no grey in his black hair, so he was still quite young, in his early thirties perhaps, and she wondered what his life had been like to give him that hard-edged cynicism so early. The woman was definitely older. Beautiful and holding. Not all the clever make-up in the world could hide the softness beginning to blur her neck or the slight boniness of her heavily beringed hands. Gigolo and wealthy consort? It suited Grace in her present mood to imagine the worst of the world in general and her unwanted companions in particular. It helped mitigate some of her own shame. She wasn't aware of the freezing contempt in her icy glare until she was caught out by a brief black glance. She jerked her eyes away, blushing.

'Are you sure it's not getting too warm in here for you?'

Grace couldn't even respond to his politeness; her throat was too clogged with embarrassment. The minutes seemed to crawl by. It wasn't just too warm, it was getting unbearably hot! The coat was more appropriate for a winter in Siberia than a marginally frosty Auckland in July. Auckland winters were more wet than cold anyway, and just keeping a coat like this dry in the city's humid environment would be more trouble than it was worth. Grace could feel herself gradually wilting as she enviously watched the man remove and fold his jacket and tie and loosen his collar and cuffs while the woman discarded the embroidered bolero which she wore over her very low-cut sleeveless green dress.

Grace's hands grew sticky in the silk-lined pockets, her face feeling hotter and hotter by the minute. She could actually feel the trickles of sweat rolling down the backs of her legs and melting into her black leather pumps. She no longer leaned against the wall of the lift, she sagged. A brief call from the newly arrived engineer with the message that they'd be freed in no more than twenty minutes brought little relief. In twenty minutes Grace feared she would be a puddle on the floor. Her main worry was that she would faint and be utterly helpless. And what if Steve was there when the lift doors opened? Grace needed to be conscious and prepared to act fast.

She couldn't even raise a haughty defence when the woman, seemingly irritated by her escort's increasing glances in Grace's direction, started on again about the evils of the luxury fur trade.

Grace was beyond caring. She had retreated to a place of cool sanctuary. The world of her imagination had always been vivid and a wonderful defence against the alternating boredom and harsh demands of her childhood. She closed her eyes and drifted there now, enjoying a cool evening on the Nile, dipping her fingers into the moonlit waters, lifting her face to the sweet night breeze that feathered over her skin.

The feathering was almost like a physical caress.

'This is ridiculous. Why don't you take the damned thing off before you really pass out? Nobody's going to steal it from you!'

Grace opened her weighted lids with difficulty, vaguely registering that the cool touch had been real, the brush of masculine knuckles against her fevered cheek. Black eyes were like the smooth wet stones on the banks of the Nile, dark and glistening and deliciously chilled to her heated senses. Her dreamy gaze immersed itself in his hypnotic coolness. She smiled gratefully, utterly lost in her sensual response to the graphic images flooding her mind.

'Oh, for God's sake——!' The man bit off his snarled undertone and reached for the concealed fastenings of her coat. Fascinated by the fierce intensity of his expression, it took Grace's sluggish brain a moment to realise his intention. A drift of warm air across her bare collarbone recalled her from her cooling fantasy.

'No, oh, no——!'

She was tall and correspondingly strong but she was no match for his determination. He simply ignored the pull of her hands against his iron wrist and swiftly dealt with the remaining buttons. When she tried to hold the edges of the coat together, incoherently protesting, he growled impatiently about women not knowing what was good for them and ripped them from her clutching fingers with one powerful movement.

He stood for an instant, holding the coat spread wide, the bulk of his body shielding Grace from the sight of his companion.

The instant was an eternity, long enough for his stunned black eyes to sweep down over the entire expanse of her blushing body and back up again to her feverishly defiant face, long enough to burn the image of her pale nudity displayed for him in a black silk frame into both their memories forever.

Then the whole world went blessedly dark.

CHAPTER TWO

GRACE BLAIR pressed her hands over her eyes, feeling the hard bones of her skull indent her soft palms. Her elbows supported on the polished rimu desk-top, she leaned into the compression of her fingers, trying to squeeze away the images that had haunted her for the last four months.

They popped into her mind at the most inopportune moments, like now, when she was supposed to be deeply involved in unravelling the mysteries of high finance. They crept up on her when she least expected them, disrupting her concentration and driving her mad with their persistence.

What must he have *thought*? she groaned inwardly, probing the wound. Oh, she could guess exactly what he had thought. It had been right there in those expressive black eyes as they had raked over her body with explicit thoroughness: the recoil of shock at the discovery that she was wearing nothing beneath the luxurious fur coat except for a pair of tiny white cotton panties, the slicing instant of cruel speculation swiftly consumed by a ferocious flare of male lust. His burning gaze had poured down over her pale, bare skin like thick, dark honey, coating every inch of her with a searing sensual awareness. Grace had blushed from top to toe, and to the very core of her woman's being.

She should, of course, have immediately snatched back the initiative, along with the edges of her coat, but she had been as stunned as he, transfixed by that all-encompassing look, incapable of the smallest sign of outrage. She had stood there, practically flaunting herself like some shameless hussy off the streets! Those few moments of actual time had stretched into an eternity in her imagination.

Grace shuddered and took a hasty sip of the rapidly cooling coffee on her desk, trying to force her attention back on to the papers demanding her attention. But, as usual, trying to hold back the tide of memory was useless.

She didn't even have the reassurance of knowing that she had quickly redeemed her modesty. When the lights in the lift had failed with such timely suddenness, it wasn't Grace who had restored the tatters of her dignity, it was the stranger. Without a word he had swiftly reversed his actions, firmly rewrapping her coat and doing up the buttons to her chin with surprising deftness.

The lights had flicked on again a minute or so later and the lift had jolted back into motion. By that time the stranger was back at his devoted companion's side, a picture of cynical remoteness.

Grace had taken one horrified peep at his unrevealing countenance and averted her flushed face. She couldn't face the knowing look in those male eyes, the disdain, or, worse, the contempt. What a delicious story this would make for him to retell to his male cronies over a few drinks. Would he laugh about it with the redhead over dinner? Or would he save it until later...much later...perhaps when they were in bed, a titillating amusement to be used as an added form of stimulation...

When the doors had opened on the ground floor Grace had fled as though the hounds of hell were at her heels, rushing out of the building and hurrying several blocks before she had dared stop to hail a taxi. She had flung herself into the dim anonymity of its interior and burst into tears of mingled humiliation and rage. She had never felt more alone in her life. She had cried miserably all the way back to her apartment, much to the dismay of the kindly taxi driver.

Although she knew that Steve would, for the sake of his own interests, keep quiet about her presence in his studio that night, Grace had been terrified that the incident in the lift would leak out and that she would somehow be identified with it. As if she didn't have enough problems! So for a few weeks she had been a fugitive, ducking between home and office swathed in scarfs and her practical blue trench-coat with its collar turned up, for all the world as if she had committed some scandalous crime. Only gradually had she realised that her paranoia was ridiculous. Auckland had a population of hundreds of thousands and the incident had occurred over on the North Shore, where she rarely ventured. It was highly unlikely that she would ever see the two strangers again and even if she did she would survive the embarrassment. She would laugh it off as a joke. Dammit, why should she cringe and cower because some men were unprincipled lechers?

It had also taken several weeks before she had been able to enter a lift again without suffering an attack of panic. Even now it took a positive effort of will before she could force herself to walk into any lift that was already occupied by a man. Fortunately the suburban building that housed Blair Components was only six storeys high and no one saw anything odd in the fact that the founder's widow often used the stairs as a way to keep fit.

Grace rubbed her heated temples, furious with herself for getting so uptight about such a silly little incident. She knew without looking in a mirror that her face must be pink. Twenty-six years old and she was suffering from hot flushes! If only she hadn't been so naïve and trusting when Steve had approached her... But then, that had always been her problem. In spite of her surface sophistication, she had a tendency to unworldliness that made her appallingly vulnerable to the discerning cynic. But that was all going to change. From now on Grace Blair was going to be one of the cynics herself, controlling events around her rather than being manipulated by them!

'How are you doing?'

Grace's pretty fantasy of herself as a power-hardened business mogul collapsed as she met the enquiring brown gaze trained on her from the doorway. She sighed guiltily.

'Not too good, I'm afraid. I can't make head nor tail of most of this stuff.' She slapped a frustrated palm down on to the papers in front of her.

'Would you like me to explain it all over again?' Neville Conway tucked the folder he was carrying under his arm as he joined her at the desk. He was a slender man of medium height, and his thinning brown hair and eyes always brought Jonathan to mind. It had been a kind of joke among them all, how alike Jonathan Blair and his accountant were, although Neville was almost a decade older. Grace felt a fresh pang of loss and struggled to overcome it.

'I *should* be able to understand it!' she said, frustrated as ever by her inability. 'You said it was all fairly straightforward...'

'To an accountant, yes.' Neville was always so patient with her that it made her feel doubly slow-witted. 'Don't worry about it, Grace; it'll come with experience. You're expecting too much of yourself. It's only been seven months since Jon died. No one expects you to work miracles——'

'Jon evidently did,' Grace said wryly, picking up the gold pen that she had given Jonathan on their first wedding anniversary—her twentieth birthday. At the time she had still been slightly dazzled by her good fortune and the totality with which a whirlwind three-week courtship had changed her life. In the twinkling of an eye it seemed she had gone from a hard-working model under the thumb of her dominating mother to pampered wife of a wealthy businessman.

'Is that what you really think?'

'I don't know!' Grace threw down the pen and swung moodily in her chair. 'I don't know what was in his mind when he made that incredible will. I mean, he always said that he didn't *want* me to work. That's why I gave up modelling. And he *never* discussed the business with me, not in any detail. Then he does this...!' Her hand swept around the office that had once been her husband's undisputed kingdom.

'Jon did tend to play his cards too damned close to his chest,' Neville conceded with a frown. Even he had been appalled to realise just how completely Jon had concealed his business problems from his wife. 'But then, he didn't expect that that will would be executed for years! He was only forty—he kept himself fit, he didn't smoke or drink and he had no family history of heart ailments. He was the *last* person you would expect to have a heart attack. When he left you the business and directed that it continue to be run as a private family concern he was probably thinking in terms of a son being in charge...'

The pain twisted like a knife inside Grace's chest. Since Jon's last will and testament necessarily meant that Grace was now a family of one she was acutely aware of the bitter irony of his legacy. Their childlessness had been the major disappointment of their six-year marriage. Although the piercing anguish of her initial grief had passed, along with the grinding depression that for a while made her doubt her own desire to live, she still missed Jon with a dull, constant ache that never left her.

'I'm sorry, I didn't mean to upset you.'

'You didn't.' Grace summoned a smile at Neville's stricken look. 'You're probably right. He was so proud of having built up this company from nothing. He'd be appalled if he could see me floundering around——'

'You're not floundering,' Neville told her sharply. 'You're doing the best you can in difficult circumstances. Don't underestimate yourself, Grace. That's your biggest problem, you know. A lot of women would have cracked under the kind of strain you've been under. Not only did you have your own grief to cope with, but there was the shock of discovering that except for the company you were virtually penniless——'

'It wasn't quite that bad, Neville,' Grace defended wanly.

'Near enough,' Neville sighed. 'Almost every asset in his estate turned out to be a liability. Even the cars were only leased, and it was damned irresponsible of him to cash in his insurances without telling you——'

'He wouldn't have seen it that way. He would have seen it as protecting me,' Grace said quietly. Jon had eagerly shared his victories with his young wife, but never his failures. 'He thought he could work his way through his problems without me ever having to worry about them. I loved him, Neville, pig-headed pride and all...'

'I know.' Neville returned her loyal smile with a wry one of his own. 'But that pig-headedness is part of the reason for our troubles. I *told* him that it was dangerous business practice to keep confidential information inside his head instead of committing it to the files, but he refused to change. If he'd put everything down on paper then we would have had a much clearer picture of the state of the business when he died and his will wouldn't have taken so long to go through probate. As it is, you had to wait months for legal title while all those damaging rumours about the company's viability were zinging about. Thank God you managed to reassure our employees and keep the flag flying. You might not know exactly what you're doing but you always manage to do it with great flair...'

'Yes, well, that's the only thing I *am* really trained for,' said Grace, ruefully accepting the backhanded compliment. 'Looking confident at all costs. I just wish I *felt* more confident. I thought I could make up in determination what I lacked in formal education. But I'm *still* making the most stupid, elementary mistakes...'

'You're doing fine, Grace,' Neville reiterated. 'Some people have an instinct for figures, other people have to work harder at it.'

Grace's blue eyes darkened with a stubbornness that was a newly acquired characteristic. Neville was too kind with her, that was part of the problem. She only hoped he wouldn't be offended by what she had done without first asking his advice. 'I'll work as hard as it takes. I owe it to Jonathan to make sure his company doesn't fail——'

'But not at the expense of your own happiness. You know he wouldn't have wanted that.'

'I'm not unhappy...' Grace wasn't so sure that Neville was right. She had been a tiny bit jealous of Jon's devotion to his beloved company. Sometimes it had seemed that it meant more to him than she did. Only now was she beginning to understand the nature of the demands of the business on his time and energy. 'I'm just confused. I've got a brain—it's a bit rusty, that's all. You've been great at showing me the ropes but, well ... I've decided that it's time I got extra professional help, so last week I enrolled in a night-school course of accountancy and business studies!'

She met Neville's surprised gaze with a trace of defiance. She had been brought up to consider her looks, not her brains, as her sole useful asset, and everyone around her had apparently thought the same.

'Well, if you need any help with your homework, let me know.' Neville's smile was slightly stiff and she knew that he was a little offended.

'I'm sure I will.' Grace was relieved he didn't ask how the first lesson had gone. Her study skills were as rusty as her brain. Reliant on her earnings as a child model, her mother had withdrawn Grace from school as soon as she was fifteen in order to guide her into full-time modelling, so it was a long time since she had opened a textbook or written an essay. If she was having trouble with the introductory lesson she hated to think of what travails lay ahead of her!

'In the meantime, what are we going to do about today?'

'The meeting with Gregory?' Neville's brown eyes narrowed with caution. 'Stonewall. Wait until we know exactly what he wants. That's the great advantage of being a privately owned company—we don't have to worry about meeting any disclosure requirements.'

Grace couldn't help shivering slightly as she thought of this latest threat to her fragile business confidence. Ever since Jonathan's death, business rivals had been snapping at Blair Components' heels, pestering Grace with offers to buy even before the company was legally hers to sell. She had been both angered and offended by their callous attitude to her bereavement, caught on the raw by their condescending assumption that she was more interested in money than preserving her husband's memory.

'When's it all going to stop?'

Neville didn't have to ask what she meant. 'Never. If you're weak you attract the scavengers; if you're strong you attract the hunters.'

'And what's Scott Gregory?'

'Both. Either. A survivor. A law unto himself; that's what makes him more dangerous than the others—he's not predictable. You have read that background I had typed up, haven't you? Gregory has won and lost several fortunes on the stock exchange. He's a gambler and by all rights he should have been wiped out by the market crash but somehow he managed to emerge even stronger than before. Since then he's concentrated solely on hostile acquisitions in the electronics industry, so you can bet he's not calling on us simply for a friendly chat.'

'Why do I have to meet him at all?' Grace felt a familiar nervous flutter in her throat. 'If he's all that dangerous, wouldn't it be safer if you handled him?'

'Maybe. But he specifically asked for you and we can't afford to offend him. He's powerful enough to destroy us if he wants to—he's done it before to other companies. The man is a piranha. If he scents blood things could get vicious, so we need to convince him that you're invulnerable—totally and confidently in command of yourself and the company.'

'Oh, right. In other words, I'm a superwoman,' said Grace wryly.

Neville didn't even smile, a measure of his nervous state. 'He claims to have had some sort of verbal agreement with Jonathan about an involvement in the company, and in the last year he's taken over three of the companies that we have major standing supply contracts for... one of which is shortly up for renegotiation. He may intend to hold it over our heads. We also have a big contract with his main competitor which is coming up for renewal. Maybe that's what he and Jonathan talked about. On the other hand he may just be on a reconnaissance mission, to reassure himself of our good faith.'

'But what if Jon *did* make him some sort of promise about buying into the business?' said Grace slowly.

'Do you really see Jon inviting some hot-shot twenty-nine-year-old entrepreneur who doesn't know the meaning of tradition or loyalty into Blair Components?'

'No, I suppose not...' Jon had believed wholeheartedly in old-fashioned virtues and principles. He had treated his employees as part of an extended family, always welcoming their input of ideas and opinions, maintaining a shrewdly paternalistic attitude that had kept staff poaching by other companies to an absolute minimum. 'But if they did business together——'

'Oh, I'm sure Jon respected Gregory's success, but when I said that he and Jon knew each other I didn't mean that they were friends—in fact, I got the impression that there was quite a bit of rivalry between them. The fact that Jon never invited him home to one of your famous dinners must tell you that he didn't regard him as a suitable acquaintance.'

Grace smiled wistfully. Perhaps partly due to his jealous awareness of the thirteen-year difference in their ages, Jon had preferred their social life to revolve around their home, where he could pick and choose the guests. 'I suppose not. But I don't think any man is *entirely* bad... Maybe Mr Gregory has quietened down with maturity...'

Neville gave a groan of irritated amusement. 'Don't go soft-hearted on me now, Grace. The man will eat you alive. For all we know, he might be the one who started the current crop of rumours about the viability of Blair, to try and soften us up.'

'Do you think so?' Grace frowned as a flare of possessiveness ignited her fighting instincts. She had been thinking of herself as merely a caretaker-owner, standing in for Jonathan, but now she realised with a secret thrill that this was solely *her* company. It was *her* reputation and self-respect that were on the line here. Her mouth compressed into a straight line that disguised its fullness. Unconsciously her face drained of its soft uncertainty and acquired the professional rigidity that she used to mask her inner thoughts.

'I wouldn't put it past him. From what I've heard, he's as cold-blooded as they come and a total cynic. People admire him and envy him but I've never heard anyone claim to actually *like* him. He's pretty much a loner, answerable only to himself.'

'Well, if Mr Piranha Gregory thinks he can force us to the negotiating table he's in for a shock.' Grace forced herself to be realistic on the heels of her bravado. 'What happens if he starts asking me awkward questions?'

'Except for those areas we discussed, stick to the yes and no routine... it always drives them crazy!' Neville's brown eyes twinkled at the remembrance of past encounters with arrogant businessmen who had confidently expected to bamboozle Jonathan Blair's pretty young widow. The stoic endurance and patient self-discipline that every model developed as a defence against the crippling boredom of her profession had proved an unexpectedly brilliant negotiating tool. With Neville at her elbow, Grace's necessarily taciturn approach to business had resulted in her acquiring a thoroughly undeserved reputation for being a shréwd opponent. That reputation was the reason for her need to attend an obscure local high school rather than a professional college for her business classes.

'Watch me if you're unsure of your ground, or give me one of the usual cues and I'll play the mouthpiece. Remember that *he's* coming to *you*, not the other way around. Don't let him intimidate you or put you on the defensive. If in doubt, hit him with that haughty reserve. It's worked a charm with everyone else.'

'I get the feeling that Scott Gregory may not run with the common herd,' Grace murmured uneasily. She told herself that there was no harm in the deception they were practising. It wasn't illegal or immoral. Bluff was part and parcel of modern business practice, Neville had explained.

'He should be here by now.' Neville frowned at his watch. 'If his being late is a deliberate tactic it doesn't bode well for his threatened "amicable intent"...'

'And there I was, thinking that perhaps he'd been held up in traffic,' Grace murmured wryly. 'But I suppose the traffic wouldn't dare!'

Neville's reply was interrupted by a quick knock at the door and they both tensed. It was Mabel, Grace's secretary, holding a large buff envelope.

'He's not here yet,' she said in her crisp, capable voice as she saw their taut expectancy. 'This just arrived by courier from Scott Electronics. It's addressed to Mrs Blair,' she added in mild reproach as Neville took it from her and began to rip open the seal.

'Perhaps he's not coming,' Grace said, not trying to hide her relief at the possibility of a reprieve.

Neville was frowning at the contents. He checked the envelope again, shaking it upside down. 'There's no message,' he said, puzzled. 'Just a Press cutting.' He skimmed through it. 'And from a tabloid at that...all about Gregory...' His thick eyebrows rose. 'What on earth did he send us this for? Does he think we didn't do our own research?'

'Not that kind,' Mabel said, scanning the full-page cutting over his shoulder, pursing her lips in surprise. She was the one who had assembled the computer file on Scott Gregory from the dry details provided by the accounts and sales departments and a brief résumé from New Zealand business directories. 'We never delved as far as the social pages,' she said, a trace of disapproval crossing her middle-aged face. 'Mmmm...it must be true what they say about him and women.'

'What do they say?' asked Grace, stretching out her hand to receive the cutting from a still perplexed Neville.

'That if a woman is beautiful, available and socially active then sooner or later she'll turn up as one of Scott Gregory's ex-girlfriends. And he doesn't discriminate on the basis of colour, race, creed, marital status or age either. Look at that selection—it's practically a who's who of New Zealand society!'

Grace couldn't give a damn about the beaming bevy of beauties framing the page. Her appalled eyes were riveted on the photograph accompanying the main body

of the story. A man was smiling down at a woman on
the steps of an elegant restaurant, making a point with
expressive hands as he spoke. Grace was glad that she
was sitting down. If she hadn't been she would have
fallen over. Her bones had turned to water.

It was him.

It was the man from the lift! *And* the woman. The
photograph had obviously been taken on the very same
night because the woman was dressed as she had been
then, right down to the huge diamond studs in her
ears . . . and she hadn't looked like the kind of woman
to wear the same outfit twice!

Grace's body went into deep shock, her mind blanking
out and her vision blurring as the room weaved around
her. Her stomach churned nastily at the awful implications. She only remembered to breathe again when little
red spots began to burst in the blurry haze and her chest
suffered stabbing pains from the deprivation. She took
a deep, sucking breath, her hands clenching violently on
the neatly clipped edges of the page.

The oxygen went straight to her brain, triggering a
burst of adrenalin that instantly invoked a full-blown
panic.

The gigolo in the lift was Scott Gregory!

Worse, she was holding the proof that he knew who
she was. Otherwise why send this pointless cutting, addressed specifically to her? There was no accompanying
note but the inherent message was very explicit indeed.
It was a threat. A secret threat that he knew that only
she would understand. She closed her eyes, horrified.
She *hoped* it was still secret! She certainly hadn't told
anyone about her crass idiocy and she prayed that he
was capable of equal discretion, although the cutting
didn't reassure her at all on that score. He seemed quite
happy to flaunt his own peccadilloes in public.

Grace squinted to read the photo caption:

Loretta, Lady Marlin, forty-five-year-old widow of philanthropic millionaire industrialist Sir Steven Marlin, is the latest in a long line of ladies to fall under the spell of the Gregorian chant...

She felt a small, strengthening stab of scorn cut through her panic. Lady? Huh! No lady truly worthy of the title would seek the company of such a relentless, unprincipled wolf...

'Grace, what's the matter? You're as white as a sheet.'

Neville's tired cliché jerked Grace out of the awful pit of impending doom into which she had been slowly sinking.

She discovered that her hands were clenched in white-knuckled fists and slowly unfolded them, smoothing out the badly crumpled newspaper in an effort to compose herself. She couldn't possibly tell Neville. He was regrettably strait-laced. But, ye gods! He had told her not to let Gregory put her on the defensive!

'Nerves, I suppose,' she murmured weakly. 'I was hoping he wouldn't look as intimidating as his reputation sounds.'

'Would you like a cup of tea? It's nearly ready. I was expecting to be serving Mr Gregory by now,' Mabel offered with motherly concern and Grace nodded gratefully.

'Plenty of sugar, please,' she said grimly, aware that Mabel gave her a curious look as she left. Grace didn't usually take sugar in her tea.

She would actually have liked a good slug of restorative brandy but Neville would have been shocked if she had asked for alcohol in the middle of the day. Besides, she would need all her wits about her to get through the coming meeting!

What on earth was she going to do? Should she beg or brazen it out? Should she turn the other cheek or slap his if he dared mention that night? She obviously couldn't rely on his gentlemanly instincts! How dared he do this to her? She felt a bolt of fury stiffen her cowardly backbone. What was *he* expecting her to do? Whatever it was, she had no intention of doing it!

An unnerving situation had suddenly become a total nightmare. Scott Gregory had a negotiating ace up his sleeve, and that ace was the owner of Blair Components!

CHAPTER THREE

'AND this, of course, is Scott Gregory...'

Grace took a deep calming breath as she dropped Mike Patrick's hand, turning away from the flattering admiration in the lawyer's eyes to meet the gaze that she had been assiduously avoiding ever since Neville had ushered the two men into the room.

The hand that she held out was steady as a rock, her expression relaxed, her self-possession complete as she bravely embraced unwelcome reality... a man every bit as big and aggressively attractive as she had remembered.

'Mr Gregory.' Her mother had sent her to an elocutionist when she was fifteen, to school the natural feminine lightness of Grace's speech into a distinctive huskiness that was supposed to be more attractive. In times of stress Grace was inclined to forget but now she was thankful for the added authority that she felt the artificially deep tone gave her.

Unfortunately today she had worn low heels, not wanting to tower over Scott Gregory should he turn out to be of average build. A lot of men felt hostile towards a woman they felt was trying to dominate them with her size. As a result she had to tilt her chin quite appreciably to look up into Scott Gregory's face and what she saw there was not reassuring.

Once again she felt the shivering impact of those deep-set black eyes. Helplessly she was reminded of the last time he had looked at her with that faintly contemptuous speculation. His mouth was curved in a caustic smile of greeting that told her he was going to enjoy making her squirm. She decided to pre-empt his pleasure.

'I can hardly say it's a pleasure to see *you* again,' she murmured wryly, giving him a small rueful smile that was as composed as her words, feeling a small tug of satisfaction as she saw the slight narrowing of his eyes.

'You've met before? You never said...' Neville, who was supposed to be her ally, put her even more firmly on the spot.

'No, well, it was a singularly embarrassing situation——'

'Oh, but *I* wasn't embarrassed at all...' Scott Gregory's voice was as smooth and controlled as her own, but it contained a stingingly provocative amusement that was like a slap on the face.

'——and we weren't actually introduced,' she continued evenly, as if he hadn't interrupted, clinging grimly to her poise.

'In fact, you *could* say that you only provided the bare essentials...'

The light mockery of his words contrasted starkly with the harsh inflexibility of his expression. The coal-black eyes smouldered with grim triumph. Any hope that he would give her a gentlemanly benefit of the doubt over the incident vanished like smoke in the wind.

Grace sighed. She thought wistfully of her husband. Jon would have been absolutely furious with her for putting herself at risk but after delivering a severe lecture on her stupidity he would have acted with his usual protectiveness to make sure there were no unpleasant repercussions. Now she only had herself to rely on, and the unflattering truth.

'We were trapped in a lift together one night...' The words were delivered with just the right degree of bored amusement but they sounded vaguely compromising in themselves, so Grace added hastily, 'Mr Gregory and Lady Marlin and I——'

'Oh, Grace, how awful for you.' Neville frowned his genuine concern. 'Did you panic? Claustrophobia is nothing to be embarrassed about. Grace has developed a recent dislike for small enclosed spaces,' he explained to the other two men with a gruff aggression that dared them to make a disparaging comment on her weakness.

Stoically Grace decided that it was better to get it over with than flounder around trying to be diplomatic. 'I'm afraid I——'

'I'm sure Mrs Blair has an excellent reason for her aversion...to lifts in particular. But no, she didn't panic. Quite the reverse. She handled herself with quite stunning aplomb. I found it most...revealing...'

Grace's dogged determination faltered at the relentlessly deliberate taunting. Dammit, he had forced her to this point; why didn't he let her get on and tell it *her* way? Her mask of composure slipped as she flashed him a briefly tempestuous scowl, her wide blue eyes darkening to a stormy navy with the tumultuous emotions that she had learned in early childhood to keep sternly repressed. She hadn't been allowed the luxury of tears and tantrums like other children and before she had learned to internalise the release in her vivid imagination she had sometimes felt like exploding with a wild frustration that she could neither explain nor understand. Now her imagination dealt her a gloriously satisfying picture of this man as a grubby, grovelling peasant whose powerful physique was no match for the forces commanded by his majestic sovereign. Oh, she would make him pay for his insolence...not with physical pain, for Grace's tender heart found no pleasure in sadism...but by crushing his pride, controlling him, humiliating his masculinity with her pity, making him beg for the mercy of her favours...

Favours?

Grace blanched at the unexpectedness of the ambush. Where had that thought come from? The very idea of any sexual involvement with a man as cold and hostile as Scott Gregory was utterly repellent. To her horror, the source of her bemusement was contemplating her with a strangely alert intensity. Under the strain of that hooded observation Grace did the unthinkable.

The ice queen blushed.

Grace felt the colour sweep across her face like sunlight across the snow. She quickly turned away and walked across to her desk as she forced herself back under control. You can do this, she told herself. Don't let him see how he threatens you. Don't give him that victory, too...

She sat down at her desk, folded her shaking hands firmly on her lap and said with cool dignity, 'I think it's time we stopped fencing, don't you, Mr Gregory? Please sit down.' Not waiting to see if he would take offence at her commanding tone, she turned to her accountant with a painful smile. 'Neville, I think I should explain that——'

'I hope you're not going to take up too much time with personal discussion, Mrs Blair. My lawyer and I do have another appointment this morning...'

Grace froze. '*You* were the one who introduced the personal element, Mr Gregory,' she said stiffly, looking straight through him as she spoke.

He smiled. 'Please call me Scott. In the circumstances formality between us is a little ridiculous.'

Grace couldn't believe it. If she was dismayed before, now she was utterly bewildered. He was backing off. But why? She didn't trust that calculated charm.

'Scott.' She inclined her head haughtily, giving his name a chilly snap. The three men had remained standing and it gave her a feeling of power to have them arranged in a row in front of her, like naughty schoolboys before the headmistress. The wicked analogy gave her the courage to continue.

'In view of your constant references, I thought it might be a good idea to explain the circumstances of our meeting so everyone might fully enjoy your cryptic utterances. Then, perhaps, you might be able to put aside your obsession with irrelevancies and concentrate on the matter at hand. I must confess, however, that I'm disappointed. Being relatively new to the business world, I thought I would gain some valuable experience from our discussions. But if this is the way you normally conduct your negotiations then your techniques have more to do with ego than sound business practices...'

Grace heard Neville suck in his breath and Mike Patrick make a small choking sound that could have been a cough or a laugh, but she didn't take her challenging blue gaze off Scott Gregory. She stiffened her shoulders, waiting for the scorching retaliation to her defiant gesture.

Instead he took her totally off guard. 'So you do agree that we have grounds for negotiation?' He stepped forward and took the chair that was square in front of Grace's desk, leaning back with one elbow casually on the other wrist, his hand propping up the jut of that determined chin. Now that he was on the same level with her Grace felt, perversely, even more threatened. His broad-shouldered, lean-hipped body looked utterly relaxed but she knew he wasn't. Like a cobra, he was coiled to strike as soon as his prey was sufficiently mesmerised.

'I agree to nothing, Mr...Scott, until I'm in full possession of all the facts,' she said repressively.

The other two men were now also sitting, and Grace shifted slightly off-centre so that she could see Neville's face without obviously moving her head.

'Very wise of you...Grace.' His hesitation before using her name exactly mirrored hers. 'The facts are what I came to present. But first, may I offer you my condolences on the loss of your husband?' His voice held the polite amount of sympathy and Grace was perforce obliged to thank him with equal politeness, unaware of the wistfulness that fleetingly shadowed her aloof expression.

'Jonathan and I have been vague acquaintances for years but only just before his death did we get to know each other more personally...'

'Hardly a recommendation for your friendship...' murmured Grace, driven by some inner devil of jealousy to reject the possibility that this man could claim comradeship with a part of her husband that she never had been permitted to share.

'I wouldn't say that we were friends,' Scott said quietly, unruffled by her cruel flare of spite. 'We were too different for that, and your husband was a cautious man, especially regarding "newcomers" to his particular field of expertise. But he initially invited *my* interest, not the other way around, as you might have reasonably assumed. We agreed to explore certain areas of mutuality. But the agreement was in principle only; for various reasons the time wasn't right for action on either side. Jonathan suggested we meet again in eight months. Those eight months are now up.'

'I'm surprised that you didn't approach us before. Surely Jonathan's death must have caused you some concern——' began Grace, to be smoothly interrupted.

'This last year has been a very busy period for me. I've been out of the country for considerable lengths of time. My advisers were aware of my interest, if not the reason for it, and would have informed me of any developments that necessitated early action. As you will appreciate, what is of major importance to *your* business may only be of minor relevance to mine.'

'I see,' said Grace stiffly, seeing very clearly the bully-boy threat underlying the polite phrasing. I am big and you are small, therefore I can please myself what I do as well as when and where... 'Naturally we're interested in any arrangements you might have discussed with

Jonathan...' Her eyes remained guarded, but she couldn't help a tiny hint of relief colouring her tone at the realisation of how far they had drifted from the dangerous subject of the lifts.

'We're not legally obligated to honour any verbal offers that might have been floated in the past,' Neville said cautiously, obliquely warning Grace not to concede her opponent any rights.

'I realise the onus of proof is on us,' Scott said drily. 'That's why I've brought tape-recordings of my meeting with Jonathan, so that you can verify the truth of the information for yourself.' Without taking his eyes off Grace he waved a hand at Mike Patrick, who briskly opened his briefcase and produced a cassette tape, which he slid across the desk towards Grace.

For the second time that morning she was taken utterly off guard. She cast a brief glance towards Neville and saw that he was as startled and wary as she. Reluctantly Grace took the tape, turning it over and over in her beautifully manicured hands as if it was likely to explode in her face. As well it might. Apart from anything else she didn't think she could handle hearing Jonathan's gruff rumbling voice again in front of strangers. The familiar ache lodged under her heart and to dispel it she looked at the flowers tucked into the dainty crystal vase on her desk, the dewy violet posy that had been delivered that morning. They comforted her and gave her confidence a boost. A secret smile that touched her lips. They told her that the world wasn't solely a dog-eat-dog place where profit was the only motive and only the most cunning and ruthless survived. It was also a world of generosity and joy where people were willing to give of themselves simply for the sake of bringing another person a little pleasure. Although the violets were symbolic of a tender sweetness that didn't really belong in the efficient, high-tech office that Jon had had designed for himself, Grace couldn't resist their fresh appeal.

'Did my husband know that he was being recorded?' She forced herself out of her protective distraction, voicing the question that she knew would be uppermost in Neville's mind.

It was Mike Patrick who answered, with a terseness that expressed his annoyance. 'There's nothing under-handed in making certain that there's an accurate record of business meetings. Everyone who deals with Scott knows that he commonly uses tape recorders when his secretary isn't there to take notes.'

Grace longed to leave it at that but knew that she couldn't. As an amateur among professionals, she had to make sure the 'i's were all dotted and the 't's crossed, that they weren't taking advantage of the yawning gaps in her education.

'I'm not interested in other people. I want to know whether my husband realised at the time that his words were being recorded.'

'Yes, he did.' Scott Gregory replied on his own behalf. 'If he hadn't known, would that have made a difference to the validity of the recording? Was your husband in the habit of making promises he had no intention of honouring without proof?'

For the first time Grace sparked into real life, a blue fire blazing in her eyes as she exploded out of her pass-iveness, slamming her hands on the desk and pushing herself furiously to her feet.

'How dare you insinuate that Jonathan had so little integrity? How dare you try and smear a fine man's reputation when he's not in a position to defend himself?' she flung at him bitterly, hating him for being alive and vibrant while her Jon was cold in his premature grave. All her hostility and emotional resentment boiled over, pouring out in a silent wave from her tense body as she sought for the words to put him in his place. 'Jon had more integrity in his little finger than you have in your entire body——'

'Grace——'

She was deaf to Neville's faint exclamation. 'He would *never* have stooped to blackmail or cheap tricks and insults to conduct his business dealings——'

'Grace——' Neville's plea had become almost plaintive.

'—nor would he have wanted to associate with anyone who did.' Grace leant forward on her fists, every inch the picture of glittering, diamond-hard confidence that she had earlier tried to project. '*I* certainly don't! My husband, *Mr* Gregory, was an honourable man. I realise you might have difficulty with such an alien concept, which is why I think that——'

'Grace!' This time Neville fairly barked it out and Grace reacted equally fiercely.

'*What*?'

There was a small fraught silence on the heels of her feminine snarl, a brief hiatus in which Grace realised how perilously close she had been to totally losing control. Neville had said that Scott Gregory would make a very powerful enemy and now he was afraid that she was going to toss away his potential friendship. If she was careful she might still be able to retrieve them from disaster, but she knew that to show any sign of discomfort now would be to admit to a weakness that the predator across the desk would take immediate advantage of.

She sat down abruptly and continued in a glacial tone that made it clear there was to be no abject apology for the spitting fury of her outburst, 'Which is why I think that any future dealings between us should be recorded by *both* parties—to preclude any possibility of errors or...*accidental* erasures. As someone as mistrustful as yourself can appreciate, Mr Gregory, the legal admissi-

bility of recorded evidence is always open to specu-
lations of tampering...'

Scott Gregory hadn't moved a muscle throughout her
furious diatribe and now the only sign that he had ab-
sorbed the subtle insult of her words was a faint flicker
of the thick dark lashes as his hooded gaze lifted from
her white-knuckled hands to her defiant face.

'Of course, I quite agree,' he said smoothly. 'I said I
didn't know your husband well, but I was well aware of
his integrity. You have my sincere apologies for letting
my temper get the better of me. My comment was made
sheerly out of pique, I'm afraid. I rather resented the
implication that I needed to seek unfair leverage by invading the privacy of others.'

Grace's ingenuousness didn't extend to manners. He
had outmanoeuvred her again. She had no choice but
to accept his handsome apology unless she wanted to
appear both childish and churlish.

'I...' The reciprocating remark stuck in her throat.
'I'm a little touchy on the subject of... of my husband.
I...it hasn't been very long since...'

He was more gracious than she, not pushing her to
finish her humbling apology. 'I quite understand.' He
paused. 'You must have loved him very much.'

She blinked at the steely quality of his unexpected
gentleness.

'I—yes, I...'

Then she remembered that, as far as Scott Gregory
was aware, a little less than three months after her husband's death his grieving widow had been flitting about
town in the semi-nude, seeking indiscriminate thrills by
flashing herself at passing strangers.

'Perhaps we should return to business,' Neville interrupted briskly, rescuing Grace from her threatening
emotions as she cast him an agonisingly blank look. 'I'm
sure it's the future we all want to concentrate on now,
rather than the past.' Having neatly dismissed the un-

pleasantness, he invited Scott to frankly explain his position so that further misunderstandings could be avoided.

'I can do that very succinctly.' Grace thought that everything that Scott Gregory did would be that way—purposeful and to the point. Like his taunting of her, her brain whispered.

Unfortunately her brain wasn't quite up to coping with his interpretation of succinct. She could follow the expected bit about trading off potential contracts with Gregory's competitors for firm pre-commitments from several of his own companies, but when he began speaking of Jon's plan for restructuring and expansion Grace was completely at sea. How could Jon possibly have been contemplating expansion at a time when his profits had been contracting?

As soon as she knew how far she was in over her head Grace relinquished some of her fierce concentration. She leaned back in her swivel chair, swinging it lightly, appearing to be listening with intent interest as Scott Gregory talked double Dutch about the financial opportunities provided by privatisation of national telecommunications. Her eyes cool and blank, she nodded thoughtfully when Neville indicated a positive response and raised her eyebrows quizzically at him when he signalled that scepticism was called for. At her appropriate response, Neville would engage openly in silent communication with her before asking his pertinent question. That the procedure seemed to irritate Scott Gregory was a bonus as far as Grace was concerned. He kept pressing her to express an opinion and she kept eluding him with the innate cunning of ignorance.

When, finally, Scott asked his lawyer to produce a recent survey on the future of New Zealand telecommunications, and requested that Mike use the office photocopier so that he could leave copies to be studied at their leisure, both Grace and Neville uttered a silent sigh of relief that they had survived the ordeal relatively unscathed.

Mike hesitated, no doubt startled at being asked to handle such a mundane office task, but Scott's pointed reference to security seemed to change his mind. Grace felt constrained to defend Mabel's reputation but she was swiftly overruled by the reigning paranoia of the electronics industry. Even Neville conceded that the fewer who knew the exact details of their meeting the better.

It was only when Grace watched Neville leave the room with the other man that she realised the awful consequences of the innocent suggestion.

Neville's rueful shrug and warning twitch of his bushy eyebrows was little reassurance. Even a few minutes was too long as far as Grace was concerned.

'Ah...would you like some more tea?' she asked, hovering over the tray that Mabel had unobtrusively placed on the coffee-table between the guest chairs some time during the meeting.

'I had coffee. And no, thank you, I had sufficient.' He stood at ease, one hand casually thrust into the pocket of his trousers, the open jacket of his charcoal-gray suit caught behind his wrist to reveal the taut plane of his stomach under the snowy white shirt.

A dark tie completed his conservative attire. The only thing that hinted at any unconventionality in his aggressively controlled appearance was his hair, which was longer than his collar, thick and straight and inky-black, as glossy and well conditioned as her own. That night in the lift it had been slicked back in an austere style which had highlighted the hard temples, bold nose and broad cheekbones. Today it was worn casual, a statement of individuality in itself. 'But do have another yourself, Grace.'

Such beautiful manners when he chose! Grace thought sourly, trying to ignore the creeping sensation of doom feathering up her spine as he stood there, unmoving, watching her try desperately to think of a safe subject until the others returned. It would be better if she sat behind her desk, she decided, firmly establishing a position of authority, and a good deal of personal space between them besides...

She took a step back and turned, but he moved casually at the same time, strolling around the other side of her desk to look out of the window at the park across the street, thereby obstructing her progress to her seat. She hesitated, feeling the walls close in on her.

'Is something wrong?'

She moistened her lips unconsciously. 'No, no...'

'He's very protective of you, isn't he?'

Her mind on other things, Grace looked blankly at his tilted profile. No, she couldn't possibly squeeze past him. 'Who?'

'Your...colleague, Conway. He didn't look very comfortable with the idea of leaving you alone with me.'

'I——'

'Doesn't he trust you?'

'It's *you* he doesn't trust!' Grace blurted out in swift retaliation, then put a hand to her mouth. She had promised she wasn't going to let him provoke her again. 'I mean, naturally he wonders about your intentions...' Her blundering was only compounding her mistake.

He turned, leaning a broad shoulder against the cold glass, his eyes narrowing to a dark glitter of amusement. 'My intentions? Whatever do you mean, Grace?' he murmured innocently.

'Your *business* intentions,' she told him stiffly, resenting his mockery.

'Ah, yes, of course. What else?' His mockery intensified. 'After all, he doesn't know that there's anything personal between us. Perhaps we should tell him that his protective instincts are misplaced. If anyone is in danger here, it's me. Who knows what outrageous action you might take to compromise my virtue——?'

'There isn't anything personal between us...and I
doubt that you have any virtues left to compromise,'
said Grace heatedly, striking out at random.

The heavy lids looked suddenly sleepily sensual.
'Compared to you, my dear, I'm a pink-cheeked
choirboy. At least I seek my pleasures privately; I don't
indulge in dangerous thrill-seeking at the risk of public
censure and scandal.'

'A choirboy!' The idea of this cynical, sensual man
being a boy at all was so ludicrous that Grace laughed
insultingly. 'Is disseminating that grubby newspaper
article your idea of preserving your privacy? But of
course I suppose you're going to claim it's all lies; you're
just a poor misunderstood innocent and all those women
were merely going out with you to share your pure and
chaste interest in hymn-singing!'

He raised a mocking eyebrow at the fieriness of her
scorn. 'You'd be surprised,' he murmured, a peculiar
glint in the dark sensual gaze. 'It's rather warm in here.
Would you mind if I took off my jacket...?'

Grace felt as if she had suddenly been dipped in boiling
water. 'Yes!'

He studied her hot face with an arrested expression.
'I wasn't proposing a striptease, Grace, I am fully dressed
underneath. I'm even wearing a vest.'

She could see the outline through his thin white shirt
and the dark shadow of body hair above it. She averted
her wayward eyes, hating him for taunting her with the
memory she had tried so hard to forget.

'Are you?'

'Am I what?' Was that her own voice, so wispy and
faint?

'Wearing anything under that prim white blouse?'

Grace closed her eyes in despair. So much for her ef-
forts to look businesslike. These days she dressed to play
down her femininity rather than emphasis it. She needed
the boost of knowing that she looked as smart and prac-

tical and as nearly sexless as she intended to be in the office. The trim dark blue suit had seemed a perfect choice, the cut helping to conceal the lush triangularity of her figure—the square shoulders and full breasts sweeping down to her narrow waist and hips and long, slender legs. But of course Scott Gregory didn't see the practical businesswoman. He never would. Whenever he looked at her he would see her as he had seen her that night...

'Grace?'

To her horror she discovered that she had unthinkingly placed her hands over the vulnerable parts of her body, as if shielding her fully dressed self against the vivid penetration of his memory. Scott had moved up on her frozen figure and clasped the arm that had folded betrayingly across her breasts, gently pulling it away.

'I'm sorry, that was extremely offensive of me.'

Grace heard the apology but she was too mortified to acknowledge it.

'I have a perverse streak of viciousness that sometimes gets the better of me. Here, sit down and have some tea. I noticed you didn't drink yours earlier...'

'No, thank you,' Grace resisted his guiding hand. 'I'm quite all right. Could you please remove your hand?'

They both looked down at the olive darkness splayed around the slender paleness of her forearm. His fingers moved but didn't withdraw.

'You have beautiful skin.'

The murmured compliment and tiny, feathering caress had the effect of drenching cold water on Grace's fevered shock. She pulled herself out of his grasp. He looked full into her face, letting her see the brutal male hunger she had seen once before on his face. But this time he deliberately allowed it to linger, frightening her with its strange intensity.

'In fact, you're a beautiful woman all round...'

He meant all over. Grace lifted her chin bravely. She wasn't fool enough to be flattered by his attention. There was only one reason a man complimented a woman he clearly despised!

'So I've been told before.' Her tone told him she hadn't been impressed then and wasn't now. 'If you don't mind I'd like to sit down at my desk——'

'Are you afraid of me, Grace?'

His gall—or was it deliberate obtuseness?—infuriated her into spitting out the ugly truth. 'Of course I'm afraid of you! Isn't that what you intended me to be?'

He tilted his head. 'I thought so, yes; now I'm not so sure.'

'Really? How awful for you,' said Grace sarcastically, becoming giddy as he rang the changes on her emotions, struggling to maintain the defence of her justifiable anger. 'You acted like a complete bastard from the moment you walked into the room——'

'That's because I am——'

'What?' she snapped shortly.

'Illegitimate. I didn't find out who my father was until my mother died when I was eleven.'

Grace felt the bile sizzle in her stomach. Did he know? Had he had her investigated so thoroughly? Did he think to so easily play on her sympathy for a fellow-traveller?

'So you're a victim of your own birth: how tragic. I suppose you decided if you had to be a bastard you might as well be the biggest of them all.'

She had never been so cruelly insulting in her life. She wouldn't have been surprised if Scott Gregory had ripped her to verbal shreds for her foul-mouthed callousness, as he was fully capable of doing, but instead he shattered her with his laughter.

His laughter was deep and relaxed, and all the more shocking for being thoroughly genuine. Where was the cold savagery that he had earlier exhibited? Grace didn't know or trust this new Scott Gregory. 'Something like that. And you're the cold-hearted, hard-nosed bitch they say you are!'

'Exactly!' She felt on safer ground fielding his insults than his appallingly unpredictable and totally inexplicable playfulness. 'Remember that. Just because you got me at a temporary disadvantage don't think that gives you any right to manipulate me or my company,' she told him frostily.

'Ah, yes, your company. The company you run so ruthlessly and so well, so calmly and competently...'

'Well, *your* first attempts to manage a business were nothing to boast about...' She targeted the greatest folly of his life, courtesy of the article he had so kindly sent her. 'At least I haven't driven us into bankruptcy——'

'Or been driven ... yet ...' He was not ashamed of his failures any more than he was boastful of his myriad successes since.

Grace felt a reckless surge of fury. 'Is that a threat?'

'I don't think I have to bother to utter threats, do I, Grace? I'm a threat to you just by *existing* ...'

More than he knew. Grace looked down to discover that she was nervously arranging the violets in the crystal vase. The silence stretched interminably as she concentrated on the mindless task.

'Did he give those to you?' His voice was as thin and quiet as the blade of a stiletto, slicing to the heart of her silence.

'Who?' It seemed impossible, but his eyes had become even darker, blacker than black as they sought to penetrate her defensive abstraction.

'Your protector—Conway?'

Grace hesitated. 'No.' But her momentary uncertainty made the denial ring hollow.

'A strange sort of flower to give a cold-hearted bitch of a business colleague ...'

Grace stiffened, her hand briefly cupping over the tiny purple heads as if to protect them from his brutal crudeness.

'More like the kind of flower one gives a lover...'

Grace reared back. 'If you're suggesting that Neville and I——'

'Are you?'

'*No!*' She didn't need to answer; the revulsion of feeling was there in her expression for him to read and interpret. 'Look, my personal life is none of your business,' she began raggedly. 'They're just flowers, for goodness' sake!'

'But they obviously have some very strong associations for you. Did you know how often you smiled at them during the meeting? Sometimes I got the impression you weren't listening to the proceedings at all...'

'I tend to look around while I'm thinking,' said Grace guiltily. 'Of course I was listening.'

'Good, then perhaps you can clarify a few points that I didn't quite understand...'

She froze. 'I...I'd rather wait until the others got back...'

'I'm sure you would,' he murmured. 'How will you know what to do or say if Conway isn't here to coach you?'

'I don't know what you're talking about,' Grace blustered desperately, her worst fears realised.

'No, and that's the problem, isn't it, darling? You really don't know what the hell you're doing! You're a mere babe in the woods. That you've survived this long is sheer luck...and maybe a good dose of pure reckless nerve.' His gloating confidence was a crushing blow, the amused indulgence in his voice more of an insult than his angry contempt would have been.

'Don't call me darling,' she gritted fiercely, wondering what on earth had happened to her legendary cool.

'Sorry, was I being condescending?' She *hated* the ease with which he always apologised, the divinely calculated, infuriating mock-innocence with which he taunted her. 'It must be aggravating for such a talented and experienced businesswoman to be treated with paternalistic indulgence by male arrogance,' he agreed gravely.

'It's annoying for any *person* to be treated that way,' she lashed back. 'For your information, my *luck* and *nerve* are being backed up by intensive on-the-job training and an extensive study programme——'

'You're studying? What? Where?' He displayed an irritating interest. She bit her lip, cursing her smarting pride for the indiscretion. 'I hope it's a properly accredited course at a reputable institution——'

He probably thought she was at university level. Grace shuddered at the thought of his finding out just how basic her 'extensive' study programme was. 'Mr Gregory—Scott—I don't know what gave you the impression that I'm incompetent to handle my own affairs——'

'I didn't suggest you were incompetent, merely grossly inexperienced,' he said mildly. 'In the circumstances you handled yourself incredibly well. Your clever choreography with Conway might have worked, too, if I hadn't already been pre-primed to explode the ice-widow myth. The psychology of business negotiation was my university thesis, you know, and I've always been a keen interpreter of body language. For example, folding your arms so tensely like that tells me that you're feeling both vulnerable and defensive. You'd like nothing more than to lash out physically at me but you know you have to maintain a submissive attitude in order to salvage what little control you have over the situation——'

'All right, you've made your point,' Grace interrupted him rigidly before he pulled her confidence totally to pieces. How was she going to tell Neville that she had failed? Not only herself and him, but Jon, too...

'Well, now...' Scott accepted his victory with a wolfish smile. 'As I see it, I have a twin advantage here. I am in possession of certain facts that could cripple your professional reputation——'

'It's not fact, it's just your *opinion*——' Grace made a last-ditch effort to reject his confidence-sapping will.

'In the small, incestuous New Zealand business community my opinion *is* fact.' Scott's steely-soft correction was not an idle boast, she knew. 'To continue: not only have I the potential to ruin your business standing, but I could also cause a very similar crisis of ugly speculation and rumour about your private life. Separately the damage to your reputation would be painful but possibly containable, but if the twin revelations burst upon the public imagination together or within days of each other you might find that you will never escape the delicious stigma of notoriety. Whatever you do thereafter will be news, to be dragged up and gossiped over again and again whenever the tabloids run short of fresh meat——'

'What do you intend to do?' Grace asked shakily, her skin crawling at the image he thrust upon her.

'Certainly not what *you* expect,' he murmured mockingly. Even if Scott's other demons hadn't been recklessly riding him, his intellectual curiosity alone would have marked her out for exploitation. Grace Blair had something he wanted, badly enough to sacrifice a great deal else for it.

'I don't expect anything from you,' she told him proudly.

'Of course you do.' He stirred his hand through the violets, loosening the bunch, rolling a single stem between his blunt fingers. 'You expect me to screw your company to the wall in order to satisfy my ego and avarice...' Grace paled at his cruel smile. 'But I would hate to think that I was so sadly predictable. So I'll be magnanimous instead...for a price.

'What will you give me, Grace, if I let you off the hook this time?' He brushed her stunned, half-open mouth with the tiny bloom he had selected as he continued with his outrageous proposition.

'What personal service would you be willing to perform to persuade me to keep all your naughty little secrets to myself...?'

CHAPTER FOUR

GRACE stared grimly at the incomprehensible doodle that adorned her notepad.

Why did these things have to happen to her?

She slumped more deeply into her chair. She was in the back row, but as far as she was concerned she wasn't back far enough. She'd have liked to be a hundred miles away from the wretched classroom.

It wasn't that her essay had been torn to shreds, first by the teacher and then by the eager criticisms of the rest of the class. It wasn't that the handing out of last week's test results had made her feel like a mental midget. No, her desire to learn was stronger than her pride, and she had survived worse assaults on her confidence.

But for her pathetic failures to be paraded in front of Scott Gregory...that was too much to bear!

Through the forest of heads in front of her Grace grimly glimpsed his pacing form. He spoke fluently and well. His subject was group dynamics and he had certainly tuned in to the group dynamics of *this* class; they were with him all the way. Everyone except Grace.

What wretched coincidence had led the dour Mr Peterson to invite the one man whom Grace had vowed to avoid at all costs to be guest speaker in his class? And what horrible twist of fate had led Scott Gregory to agree?

By sitting at the back and keeping her head down Grace usually avoided being called on to answer questions or read out her work. Tonight of all nights Mr Peterson had asked her to stand and deliver. Until then she had thought she might be able to escape Scott's notice. Certainly in his sweeping glance across the attentive class when he entered the room he had not appeared to recognise the hunched figure with pale face at the end of the back row.

In her eagerness to fit in with the casualness affected by the rest of the disparate members of the class Grace had abandoned her normal stylish elegance in favour of jeans and sweat-shirts on class nights, although her flair with accessories wasn't so easily subdued. She wasn't even wearing make-up. She had tried so hard to blend into the woodwork like a proper student that tonight she felt all the old, faintly panicky sense of inferiority she had always experienced in the classroom. When she had stood up to read she had stumbled like a schoolgirl who had barely mastered English, let alone the subject she was attempting to cover. She hadn't looked at Scott but no doubt he was now feeling insufferably smug and contemptuous.

'In business, knowledge is power...' To her horror, Grace saw out of the corner of her eye that Scott was prowling down her aisle. He stopped just in front of her desk. Two strong hands planted themselves on her desktop, the sleeves of his dark suit hiking to reveal immaculate white cuffs fastened with wafer-thin gold cufflinks and a multi-function watch on his right wrist. He wasn't going to let her avoid him any longer. Her scowling gaze reluctantly climbed the amber silk tie that brushed her desk, up past the elegant knot at the throat, over the dark-shadowed jaw and faintly cruel patience of his mouth, up to the bold black eyes.

'Don't you agree?' he asked softly.

'About what?' she said flatly, reduced to fighting him with dumb insolence.

'That knowledge is power?'

If that was the case then Grace was the weakest of the weak. She shrugged.

'I suppose so.' She could feel every eye in the class glued to her uncomfortable face.

'You only *suppose*?' he mocked. 'Don't you have the courage of your convictions...Miss—er...?

Oh, he was really laying it on with a trowel.

'Randell...' offered the weedy young man at the next desk helpfully. 'Grace Randell.'

'Miss...Randell?' Only Grace heard the faintly mocking rise in his voice and she flushed guiltily, even though she had every right to use her maiden name if she chose. Just when she thought he was going to denounce her, not only as a dunce, but also as a fraud, Scott swung away from her, apparently losing interest in his miserable victim.

Grace didn't hear the rest of his lecture, deaf to everything but her jangling confusion. Since that day in her office three weeks ago when he had uttered his breathtaking promise of blackmail she had been on tenterhooks, waiting for the other shoe to drop. Had he meant it the way she had shockingly interpreted it, as a sexual threat? Or had he just been toying with her for his own idle amusement? She had waited in vain for him to explain himself. Instead he had suddenly been conspicuous by his restraint in a matter which he had claimed that he had wanted to handle personally. He had delegated Mike Patrick to deal with any queries from Blair Components and had himself been absent when Neville and Grace had visited the impressive mid-town Auckland office of Scott Electronics. Grace had shared Neville's deep suspicion of this switch in tactics, but not for the same reasons!

When Mr Peterson called for the class to show their appreciation of the evening's guest, Grace was too busy gathering her bits and pieces together to join in the enthusiastic applause. She had hoped to take advantage of the breaking up of the class to make a clean getaway but, as all the students clustered around Scott, Doug

Peterson caught Grace just as she tried to slink out of the door.

'Grace?'

Grace hugged the leather briefcase that had been Jon's to her tightening chest and sighed. 'Yes?'

'That was a very...*interesting* essay you read out——'

'Thank you.' Grace's heart sank still further as she waited for the inevitable 'but'...

'But I wonder whether you *quite* understood the concept we were exploring here? You have a tendency to approach things from a very novel and refreshing angle but, particularly in the area of general accounting practices, it is always better to err on the side of conservatism...'

Grace nodded dutifully as he meandered on, eyeing the thinning crowd at the door, only half paying attention until Doug Peterson said something that engaged her full dismay.

'*What* did you say?'

'I said perhaps it might be a good idea to rethink the courses that you've chosen,' the older man suggested delicately. 'Perhaps you're taking on too much at once. I understand you're doing School Certificate economics and accountancy as well. This course is really designed for people who already have some grounding in business studies. It's definitely not for beginners——'

Scott was beginning to move in their direction now and Grace began to gabble, only managing to make herself sound less capable than ever. 'Oh, I'm sure I can cope. I just need to work a bit harder——'

'You're a trier, Grace, I'll give you that,' her teacher damned her eager assurances with his faint praise. 'But I only see you once a week in a classroom situation—I can't give you the kind of individual attention I think you need.'

There was a small, awkward silence, and he added kindly, 'If you're determined to stick to it, perhaps some private tuition——'

Grace grabbed at the lifeline. 'Oh, yes, if you could I'd really appreciate it.'

Doug Peterson looked a little embarrassed. 'I didn't mean me, Grace. I'm afraid I'm pretty tied up with my regular teaching duties.'

'Of course,' Grace murmured hastily, realising that she probably couldn't afford the extra time or expense of personal tuition at this stage anyway. She'd have to ask Neville, even though his excessive, pedantic explanations were more often confusing than helpful.

'Call in at the school office as you leave; they usually have a list of freelancers——'

'Yes, I'll do that.' Grace cut him off rather rudely. Scott was now standing off to one side, ostensibly reading the notes on the blackboard, but he was well within hearing and he would have no scruples about eavesdropping a private conversation.

'Good. Oh, Grace...?'

'Yes?' A tiny shrill of impatience leaked through into her voice as she turned back again, trying to mask her desperation to leave.

'If you're calling into the office, would you mind dropping this off for me while I talk to Mr Gregory? It'll probably be closed up by the time I get there.'

Conscious of the black eyes now turned in her direction, Grace almost snatched the small folder from his hands and, with head averted, hurried thankfully out. As well as giving her a cast-iron excuse to leave quickly, she now knew that there was no danger of running into Scott on her way out. Douglas Peterson had virtually just promised to keep him busy!

Since the school car park had been full when she had arrived, Grace's car was parked in a nearby side-street. The wintry wind funnelled down the gleaming black road, making her shiver. The street-light a few metres away had been vandalised so that she had to fumble in the darkness for her keys, briefly mourning the loss of the sleek coupé with the infra-red remote locking system that had had to go back to the car-leasing firm. She was paying off the small Japanese second-hand car she had purchased by hefty weekly instalments that required strict budget management, quite an achievement in itself for someone who until a few months ago had never even had to balance a cheque-book! Grace's mother had always managed her modelling income and after she was married Jon had naturally handled all their finances.

'Can I help?'

Scott had taken the keys from her cold hand and unlocked the passenger door of the car before Grace had time to get her breath back.

'You terrified me, looming out of the darkness like that,' she snapped, pressing a hand to her hammering heart.

'You shouldn't be out here on your own, anyway,' he had the gall to tell her. 'It's not exactly a salubrious neighbourhood.'

'What are you doing here, then?' Grace shot back, not willing to admit that she was more than a little uneasy about the reputation of the district in which the school was located, although the quality of the teaching had more than justified her choice. 'Slumming?'

'You might say I'm returning to old hunting grounds...'

It wasn't the answer she had expected. She clenched her teeth to stop her jaw from dropping. 'This—you lived around here?'

'Is that so difficult to believe?'

Her eyes wandered over his custom-tailored suit. But no, suddenly it wasn't difficult to believe that Scott Gregory had sprung from these reputedly wild streets.

She opened the door and tossed her briefcase on to the passenger-seat then turned, braced for an argument.

'Could I have my keys back, please? I'm in rather a hurry.'

'Certainly.' He meekly dropped them into her out-stretched hand, and she was still congratulating herself at having smoothly extricated herself from potential trouble when she got behind the wheel, and discovered Scott sitting beside her, her briefcase on his knee.

'What are you doing?'

'Coming in from the cold. That wind was chilling me to the bone.'

'Then I suggest you go and get into your own car.' It was bound to be far more luxurious than her own.

'I came by taxi.'

'I'm sure you can call one from the school.'

'That's not very friendly, Grace,' he said gently, un-nerving her further.

'But we're not friends——'

'Colleagues, then. And perhaps something more...'

A shiver slid down her spine. 'Not if I have anything to do with it,' she muttered involuntarily.

'Then you're not going to take your teacher's advice?'

Grace was instantly wary. He couldn't have talked to Doug Peterson for more than a few minutes after she had left and now she knew what the subject had been.

'I understand you're looking for a private tutor...'

In the dim interior of the car she couldn't see the expression on his face, but the soft, husky words were warning enough. The key was shaking so much that she had difficulty getting it into the ignition.

'*No*——'

'No what? You haven't even heard my proposition yet.'

'I don't need to. I know I'm not going to like it. Would you mind getting out of my car? I want to go home...'

'Hurrying home for dinner?'

'Yes, I——' She knew she had made a mistake as soon as he pounced on her admission.

'I haven't eaten either. Have you got enough for two? That's if you were planning on eating alone. But perhaps you have one of your... particular friends waiting for you?'

If she hadn't been overwrought she would have clutched at the straw, but she was oversensitive to the suggestion of promiscuity where he was concerned.

'Of course not! And no, there's not enough for two.'

'Then we'll go out to eat. I know just the place...'

'I'm not going anywhere with you. Get out of my car——'

'Or?'

'Or... or...'

'Or you'll make a fuss?' She didn't have to look at him to know he was smiling. 'But why would you do that? Surely the last thing you want to do is draw attention to yourself... to your reasons for being here... to your identity...?'

'This is blackmail,' she said shakily.

'How perceptive of you.' He wasn't only smiling; he was also laughing softly, taunting her with her helplessness. 'Now shall we find that restaurant?'

'I... I'm not dressed to go out.'

'You look fine... very young and fresh, and the restaurant is a regular haunt of mine. If they try to turn us away you can borrow my tie.'

Humour? Surely it was only nerves that made Grace want to share his grin. Young and fresh? Was that just a hungry euphemism for naïve and vulnerable? Grace started the engine and concentrated grimly on her driving. He might have manoeuvred her into sharing a meal with him, but he couldn't make her like it!

To her dismay, the waterfront restaurant was casual and friendly and the atmosphere far too cosy for Grace's peace of mind. It wasn't at all the kind of place she had

imagined Scott frequenting. When the owner came out
of the kitchen to greet the newcomers Scott responded
to the flood of welcoming Italian in the same language.
When they were seated at a tiny table for two, having
been promised two plates of the night's 'special', Grace
was driven to satisfy just a little of her curiosity.

'Are you part Italian?'

Scott took a sip of the red wine he had purchased
from the wine store next door to the unlicensed restaurant and relaxed back in his chair. He had taken off
his jacket and tie soon after they had entered the spicy
warmth of the small café.

'What makes you ask that? Because I speak a little
Italian? I speak English too but that doesn't make me
British.'

'I just wondered ... you're very dark ...' Grace was
reluctant to reveal that she had even thought about him.

'My mother was half-Hawaiian.'

'Oh!' Grace was startled and it showed.

His mouth twisted. 'Why is that so surprising?'

'I suppose ... I always think of Hawaiians as being
easygoing and good-natured and ...'

The heavy lids drooped. 'I can be very good-natured,
Grace, if only I'm given the opportunity ...' Unconsciously she shivered and suddenly the black eyes glittered with a frightening bitterness. 'But perhaps I do
have more of my father in me than I like to admit. He
more than offset my mother's frankness and warmth.
His pride was worth more to him than anything
else ... even money, which came a close second.'

'I see.' She didn't, but she wanted to. To disguise the
little flurry of compassion that weakened the walls of
her hostile resolution, Grace lowered her eyes and took
a sip of the rich ruby wine. She wasn't responsible for
whatever had happened to Scott as a child. She mustn't
let herself be tempted to see him as anything but a threat.
She took another, deeper draught from her glass. The

wine was smooth and heavy and its potency gave her courage. She raised her eyes, the softening blue cool and steady again, filled with the quizzical haughtiness that had been so alluring to photographers. 'How...interesting.' Her bored tone contradicted her words.

Instead of looking annoyed, Scott leaned forward, resting his dark-shadowed chin on a cupped hand. 'I thought you'd find it so.'

'On the principle of know thine enemy?' she enquired sweetly.

'I'm not your enemy, Grace.'

She wouldn't let him get away with that flagrant lie. '*Friends* don't try to blackmail each other.'

'I don't imagine that you make it easy for anyone to be friends with you these days. If I had made friendly overtures towards you, Grace, what would you have done?' He smiled faintly as her eyes darkened. 'Yes, you would have backed off as fast as you're trying to now. Why don't we get one obstacle out of the way, at least? Why don't you tell me what you were doing naked in that lift?'

'I wasn't naked!' hissed Grace furiously, looking furtively around, even though it was doubtful that anyone could overhear them. The restaurant was humming quietly with customers and the background music from popular operas masked any conversation from discreetly placed adjoining tables. 'In fact, I was completely covered almost from head to foot.' Why was he asking this now? He had already formed his conclusions. His contemptuous attitude when they were introduced had made that clear.

'Until I uncovered you,' he pointed out blandly. 'Do you know that, whenever I see pink rosebuds now, I think of you?'

'Rosebuds?' Grace looked at him blankly.

'Don't you remember?' he murmured softly. 'The knots of pink rosebuds that were sprigged all over your little cotton panties.'

Grace flushed deeply, unable to tear her eyes away from his hypnotically dark gaze.

'They were rather darling, practical, girlish panties. Not at all the sort of thing a vamp would wear under a thirty-thousand dollar mink. Black suspenders and a corset would have been more appropriate with that mink——'

'I wasn't trying to vamp anyone!' whispered Grace feverishly and then, suspiciously, 'How did you know it was worth thirty thousand?'

He laughed, a warm, purring sound that drew a few stray feminine glances. 'I have a good eye for quality.' His narrow mouth acquired a sensual curve. 'And I've bought a mink or two in my time.'

'I bet you have,' muttered Grace heatedly, practically squirming under his amused gaze.

'So...are you going to tell me what *really* happened that night? Or are you going to leave the details to my extremely vivid imagination?'

He was teasing her, but not with any malice. Grace didn't know whether to trust to that warmth or not. 'Why do you want to know?'

The hand that was under his chin moved to still her nervous adjustment of her knives. His palm was surprisingly soft and smooth, his fingers as they folded over her tense ones long and well shaped, their gentleness hinting at a latent strength. 'Because if you don't every time we meet you'll wonder if I'm thinking about it...*what* I'm thinking about it and about you. And believe me, Grace, there is no way you can avoid meeting me—often—if you intend to stay in the electronics business. It'll be a crippling handicap to you at every encounter. What was for me an enjoyable, if rather startling incident is quite obviously deeply unsettling and embarrassing for you. You'll never feel comfortable with me until you have a chance to explain...'

'And naturally you'll trustingly believe whatever I choose to tell you,' said Grace sarcastically.

'If it's the truth, yes,' he said simply. 'I may be rather cynical where women are concerned, but I'm not blind. I know that the truth is often stranger than fiction. If you were as brazen and reckless as your presence in the lift had seemed to indicate you would have faced me later without turning a hair, with a ready lie or pretty plea for understanding. Instead you were a curious mixture of doubt and defiance. You practically challenged me to take you down. It occurred to me that only outraged innocence would be so stupid——'

'I am not stupid!' Grace had heard that too often from photographers who treated models like dumb animals.

'Of course not,' he said soothingly, his thumb moving over hers. 'If you were stupid you'd be turning your back on this chance to set things straight...'

Grace pulled her hand away before he got a chance to feel her pulse thundering. Perhaps the truth would work in her favour. He already knew how ill equipped she was to compete with him on business terms. Why not completely disillusion him? Perhaps he would leave her alone if he knew she wasn't willing to play man-woman games—with anyone.

'I... After Jon died I started modelling again and this... this photographer I had known from before my marriage said that he was scouting for a lucrative swimsuit contract—that if the clients liked the test shots then I wouldn't have to worry about any other work for the duration of the two-year contract. He... I went to his studio and he took some shots...' Grace hurriedly took another sip of wine to wet her tight, dry throat. Her skin still crawled at the memory. The way Scott had looked at her had been flattering compared to the loathsome touch of Steve's pale eyes and sly, groping hands. 'It was all right at first, except the swimsuits got more and more flimsy and revealing, and then when he wanted me to get into a mono-kini I... we had a row and he threw most of my clothes into the bathroom and locked the door and I...I suppose I panicked. I pretended to go along with him and then while he was getting drinks I grabbed the coat to wear and ran.' She grimaced. 'The mink was for a genuine fashion layout we had done earlier that day. I think he was more terrified that I might damage or lose the coat than he was upset at my running out on him...'

'You mean he came after you?'

Staring into her wine glass, Grace didn't see the grim intensity of the expression on his face; she only heard the soft neutrality of his words.

'He came round to the house.' The big, empty mansion that the bank had swiftly claimed back. 'I didn't let him in... I just threw the mink out of the window——' she smiled unwillingly, with a tiny trace of malice '—right into the rose garden. I think he might have nicked the lining getting it out because he left cursing and swearing about insurance. He rang the next day and told me that I needn't bother trying to get another modelling job in Auckland; he'd make sure my name was mud with the agencies...'

'Could he do that?'

Grace lifted her chin. 'It doesn't matter. I didn't really want to return to modelling full-time anyway. I had enough of it as a child.'

'Then why were you interested in the contract?'

Grace hesitated. She couldn't tell him she had desperately needed a quick source of cash, so she settled for the secondary truth. 'After Jon died I was so very lonely... we never had any really close friends, you see, it was just... *us*. I needed to get out, to do something, and modelling was the only thing I was trained for.' Grace avoided the perceptive black gaze. 'I didn't know for a few months what the situation with the company was. Not long before he died Jon had told his lawyer that he had drawn up a new will himself, but there was no copy of it in any of Jon's files or at home. It eventually turned up in a bank strong-box that nobody even knew he had.'

'Did he hurt you?'

Grace was shocked. The idea was ludicrous. '*Jon*?'

'No, not your *husband*. That damned photographer!' Scott's patience was dangerously brittle.

'Oh—no, not really...'

'What does "not really" mean?' he enquired grimly. 'Did he try to rape you?'

'*No*!'

'But he touched you?'

He could see how disturbed he was making her. Why was he forcing her to go over the ugly details? 'Yes, but not...I mean he gave me a couple of bruises, that's all. I don't think he would have forced me all the way if I'd kept fighting him. He frightened me more than anything. I've never been in that sort of situation before——'

To her dismay, Scott's anger suddenly refocused on her. 'It was a damned stupid thing to do—go to his studio alone at night——'

'It wasn't night when the session started,' she said defensively. 'And I told you, it all seemed quite legitimate. He was always very nice to me in the past. I wasn't to know that this time he had anything more than business on his mind.'

'But with that nasty experience under your belt you'll be more wary from now on...you'll have the sense to realise when a man is after more than just your signature on a dotted line?'

She couldn't fail to miss the ironic amusement. *A man*. They both knew he was talking about himself. But she wouldn't give him the satisfaction of admitting it.

'Shall I break him for you?'

Grace was still trying to recover from her flushed confusion. 'Who?'

'That photographer? Shall I take the revenge that he threatened on you?'

'*No!*' She was aghast at the thought.

'Because you don't feel he deserves it? Maybe you led him on a little, out of innocence ... or playfulness?' he goaded cruelly.

She was angry now. 'No! Because it's not my right to sit in judgement. What good does revenge achieve? It only spreads the bitterness around. Anyway, if he makes a habit of it, his sins will probably find him out in the end. I don't suppose a man who acts like that is a particularly happy one ...'

'As graceful of spirit as you are of name.' Somehow the softly lyrical phrase didn't sound entirely like a compliment. 'You're going to have to harden up, Grace, if you want to survive in our business. Won't you at least tell me his name?'

The waiter had brought their food, a delicious seafood pasta in velvety sauce for Grace and a hearty beef ravioli for Scott. Bolstered by the wine and the comforting presence of the waiter, Grace regarded the man across the table steadily.

'No.'

'One day, Grace, you're going to change that negative tune. One day you're not only going to say yes to me, you're also going to say yes ... *please* ...' His rough, throaty tone, so different from his usual clipped delivery, was redolent with wickedness, his eyes glittering with laughter as the waiter chuckled openly at the suggestive wording and Grace's betraying gasp.

'The day I beg you for anything is the day that I retire to a nunnery,' said Grace crushingly.

'Oh, it's easy to beg, Grace, when you want something badly enough. Allow me to demonstrate. Please, Grace, *please* pass me the salt ...'

Grace was tempted to throw it at him. 'Salt causes hypertension,' she told him sternly.

'Then I'd definitely better not have any. My blood-pressure is high enough as it is whenever you're around——'

'Scott!'

He smiled at her kindly 'Yes, Grace?'

'Stop it.'

'Enjoying your company? How can I, after I went to such a lot of time and trouble to arrange it?'

'What do you mean?' Grace frowned at him.

'I mean surely you don't think it was sheer blind co-incidence that I turned up to lecture in one of your classes?'

Grace's laden fork stilled, halfway to her mouth. 'You mean you...?' Her voice faded as her worst fears were confirmed by his predatory smile. He was letting her know that she was being hunted. She forced herself to carrying on eating at least with the appearance of un-concern. 'How did you find out?'

'I asked.' For someone as powerful as Scott Gregory, it was as simple as that. What knowledge he couldn't acquire himself he could pay others to seek for him.

'Why? So you could embarrass me?'

'So I could understand you. And yes, part of it was that I wanted to make you aware of me, of what I am and what I can do.' Before she could question what he meant by that he was continuing. 'Actually I'm asked to lecture quite often since I've become "respectable" — mostly at business seminars, preaching to the converted. I rather enjoyed tonight's eager audience. Maybe it's something I should do regularly.'

Disconcerted by his air of sincerity, Grace pointedly turned her attention to her food. Not for the world would she tell him he would make an excellent teacher. His ego was already inflated enough!

In spite of the disturbing presence across the table, Grace discovered that she suddenly had an appetite. The food was flavoursome and filling, a pleasurable temptation to tastebuds that had been dulled by months of dutiful refuelling of her listless body. Against the odds she found herself relaxing, even laughing at Scott's stories about his recent travels overseas.

She was shocked when she finally glanced at her watch to see how late it was, and was instantly restless again.

'They must be going to close soon. Hadn't you better phone for a taxi now?' she murmured, reluctantly bracing herself for another argument.

'Gino will do that for me,' he agreed casually, signalling Gino, making his request and handing over his credit card to settle the bill before turning his suddenly grave attention back to Grace's uneasy face.

'I suggest that we start off with twice a week and see how we go from there...'

'Twice a week?'

'I'm going to help you with your lessons, remember?'

Grace hoped he couldn't see in her expression what she had thought he meant. It was her guilty conscience betraying her. Scott made her aware of her womanhood in a way that even Jon hadn't. With Jon she had felt soft and feminine and confident of his love and admiration. Scott made her tense and angry, defensive and threatened, the feelings all churned up together with an unwilling recognition of his intense masculinity.

'I don't think——'

'That you want my help? Maybe not, but you need the kind of advice and coaching that I could give you. And I'm offering it.'

'No strings attached?' Her disbelief challenged him. 'Why are you doing this? After all, it might be in your own interests if I fail my courses.'

'If I wanted to sabotage you, Grace, all I have to do is stand back and let you flounder around on your own.

Your company's not as healthy as you'd like everyone to think.'

Grace's expression chilled as she rose jerkily to her feet, the ease and humour of a few minutes ago forgotten. 'What makes you say that?'

His features hardened as he slowly stood up. 'I dig deeper than most people,' he said bluntly. 'Like it or not, Grace, I'm already firmly in your life. I have a personal stake in your future. I require your co-operation in a deal but I want it voluntarily. I have hassles enough without coping with hostility from my allies as well as my enemies.'

'Is that what you've decided I am, an ally?' Grace asked with a tinge of husky uncertainty as he shouldered back into his jacket and they moved towards the door. 'That doesn't necessarily mean that you're not *my* enemy...'

His eyes narrowed. 'That depends on what you expect of your enemies, and your... friends ... Why don't you ask yourself why you're so afraid of trusting me?'

'You expect me to trust someone who threatens me with blackmail!' Grace collected herself sufficiently to smile a goodbye at Gino as Scott signed his bill and tucked his credit card carelessly in his back pocket. Like most wealthy men, he probably rarely carried cash. Grace stepped across the threshold and gasped as she again felt the bite of the cold air.

'I don't think it's that that's making you so anxious...'

'Oh?' He was just trying to play on her insecurities, Grace told herself, clinging desperately to her poise.

'No. I think you're fighting yourself as much as you are me.'

'If you mean what I think you mean, you couldn't be more wrong,' Grace said steadily. 'I happen to be still in love with my husband——'

'Your ex-husband. He left you.'

His brutal words seized her by the throat, shattering her false calm. Grace almost choked to get the bitter words out. 'He *died*, damn you, he didn't leave me...'

'You're alone, aren't you? Alone and in need.'

'Not the kind of need you're talking about,' she said raggedly, taking a darting step towards her car, but he wouldn't let her go. He turned her back and his hand was curled around the nape of her neck, holding her there for his mouth.

It was hot and hard and hungry, his lips and teeth and tongue ravaging the softness of her startled mouth with a thoroughness that was as devastating to her senses as it was to her pride. It was a kiss of possession, a threat far more potent than any of his words had been. There was no tenderness, no apology in the greedy way he plundered her weakness. He was indulging himself, branding her with a searing taste of the sensual fire that smouldered beneath the cold purposefulness of his character. Grace was horrified at the twisted pleasure it gave her to know that she could drive him to such extremes. Even so, it was he who pulled back first.

'No!' She could barely form the word with her swollen mouth. 'Don't—Jon——'

'Jon is your past, not your future.' He pushed ruthlessly against her instinctive resistance to his will. 'There is nothing he can give you now but memories——'

'You're wrong, oh, you are so *wrong*!' cried Grace wildly, wanting to shock him as brutally as he had her, to shake his implacable confidence. 'He can give me his child!'

Scott went rigid. 'You're pregnant?' Still holding her arm, he stepped back, his gaze automatically dropping to her flat stomach, as he swore. 'No, you can't be—it's been seven months——'

In ordinary circumstances Grace would never have dreamed of revealing such deeply intimate facts about her marriage, but she was too fiercely determined to crush his ego to think straight. 'Jon and I wanted children but for some reason I had trouble conceiving, so we went to a fertility specialist last year... There was nothing physically wrong with either of us, but as part of the testing programme Jon had some of his sperm frozen. He wanted desperately to give me his baby... and he still can—all it takes is one visit to the doctor!'

So intent on their private little war were they that neither protagonist noticed the sweeping headlights that blazed across their pale faces, heralding the arrival of a taxi at the kerbside.

'My God, you wouldn't...?' Scott's expression of horror was gratifying, but Grace's triumph was short-lived, for an instant later he had mastered his instinctive recoil of distaste and taken her outrageous weapon for himself.

'If it's a baby you want, Grace, I'd be delighted to oblige,' he purred dangerously. 'Wouldn't you rather conceive one with a living, breathing, pleasure-giving male? I can promise you a much more exciting way to gratify your belated desire for motherhood than a sterile encounter with a syringe!'

Long after his taxi had gone Grace sat behind the wheel of the car, trying to will away the shaking of her limbs. How well he had mastered the Parthian shot.

Scott Gregory was master of most things he tackled. But not of her. *Never* of her!

CHAPTER FIVE

'CHRYSANTHEMUMS this week, Mrs Blair.'

Grace looked up at the beefy body in black leathers topped with a mass of apricot-coloured blossoms that was advancing towards her desk. Thick, tattooed fists were wrapped around the beribboned stems.

'I was beginning to think you'd forgotten me, Vince.' Grace put down the papers she had been loading into her briefcase as the massed chrysanthemums lowered to reveal the cocky grin she had become familiar with over the past four months.

'Nah. Had trouble with the bike.' Vince worked for his cousin, who owned a nearby florist's. He used his motorcycle side-car to make his deliveries, and a more incongruous delivery boy Grace had yet to meet.

'Mmm, these are lovely.' She felt the familiar lift that the arrival of fresh blooms always gave her. A little frivolity on a Monday to help her face the rest of the week. She made a production of searching the apricot heads. 'What, no card?'

'Must'a left it in me other suit.'

They grinned at each other. There was never a card. Even Vince's cousin didn't know who had placed the standing order for flowers; as far as he was concerned, it was just a regular cash payment direct into his bank account.

When the flowers had first starting arriving all those months ago Mabel had driven her crazy speculating on who Grace's secret admirer was. Every male visitor to the office was subject to intense study. Grace hadn't shared her fervent curiosity. She had only made enquiries in order to shut Mabel up. To find out the source of her weekly floral fillip would mean putting an end to the foolish extravagance, for she couldn't possibly continue to knowingly accept such a gift. There was also the fact that she might be disappointed if she found out who the giver was. What if it turned out to be someone she loathed? Or a mistake? What if all this time she had been receiving flowers meant for another woman? At least by being incurious she wasn't obligating herself to any real person.

'Grace, have you seen——?' Neville broke off, frowning as Vince sloped past him with a mocking salute. 'You know, it doesn't do the company any good to have people like that hanging around the offices.'

'He doesn't "hang around", Neville, and he's only here once a week,' Grace replied mildly.

They had had this argument before. She noticed how Neville had never shared the speculation about the source of her flowers, had indeed seemed uncomfortable with their very existence. Mabel had scoffed at the possibility that Grace's secret admirer could be Neville. She claimed that the man didn't have a sensitive bone in his body, but Grace sometimes wondered if his discomfort was a screen to cover his embarrassment that she might guess the truth. She agreed that Neville didn't appear to be particularly sensitive, but sometimes the people who appeared calm on the surface were those with the deepest depths.

The analogy made her think of Scott Gregory...again. She knew to her cost that under the icy exterior he projected there was a volcano of sorts—she had been alternatively chilled and burnt by both extremes since she had met him. Extremes? Yes, that description suited him. For all his cold intelligence and calm business acumen, he was a man of extremes. He would hate as violently and completely as he loved, without compromise, without mercy.

'You're seeing him tonight, aren't you?' Neville said gruffly as she placed a familiar textbook on to the rest of the contents and tried to squeeze the lid shut.

Grace didn't have to ask who 'him' was; it was implicit in every stiff, mistrustful syllable. 'It's my study night tonight, yes.'

'I still don't like it, you know, Grace. I don't like the way he's been sniffing around the company... he's a bit too interested for my peace of mind. A bit too helpful and reassuring. You can't tell me that he's helping us out purely out of the goodness of his heart, because by all accounts he hasn't got one. I know you think that you're not telling him anything he doesn't already know, but maybe he knows less than you think he does. He's already practically got us over a barrel with his offer—we don't want to give him any more leverage. What's he really up to? That's what I want to know.'

Grace would like to know, too. After having virtually blackmailed her into accepting his help and threatening her with all sorts of sexual innuendoes, Scott had thoroughly disconcerted her by turning into a relentlessly impersonal taskmaster. When he had refused to let her wriggle out of the agreement he had forced upon her she had reluctantly shown up at his office that first evening, fortified by her acute embarrassment over their last encounter and prepared to resist him with every fibre of her being. But he had ignored her sullenness. Instead of assaulting her virtue he had mercilessly assaulted her intelligence. He had demanded more from her than all her other teachers rolled together. His methods were startlingly simple and terrifyingly effective. Argument. He never let her rest, never let her feel secure in her understanding, never even let her put pen to paper in his presence. Instead they read and then he bullied her into talking. As an agent provocateur and devil's advocate he was superb. He challenged every statement she made, regardless of its truth or worth. He forced her to think on her feet, to articulate her ideas, however foolish-sounding, to defend every theory and proposition, thereby tracing it to its logical roots. To her chagrin she got to use none of the clever, cutting phrases of rejection that she had rehearsed. As suddenly as he had burst upon her dormant feminine consciousness he had withdrawn, leaving her floundering in the absurdity of her own suspicions. Perversely, she was piqued by his about-face, but the respite enabled her to recover from her violent over-reaction to his presence and begin genuinely to appreciate the mental stimulation of his undoubted intelligence.

To Grace's further chagrin, his arrogant methods had borne almost immediate fruit. In just three weeks she had acquired enough confidence to express herself both positively and negatively in her regular classes. Scott had made her see that mistakes were to be learned from, not swept under the carpet. She had been letting her own and other people's doubts about her inhibit her progress. Real learning was a process of growth and exchange, not a passive action.

She wasn't feeling at all passive later that evening as she juggled her briefcase and the flowers while she wrestled with the eccentric lock on her apartment door. Her car had stalled at a roundabout on the way home and to her fury had refused to start again. Thanks to the absence of rush-hour Samaritans, she had had to stand out in the pouring rain with the bonnet up for five minutes, before someone had stopped to help push it to the side of the road. There it had had the gall to start at the first masculine touch, gaining her black looks and choice comments about female drivers from her erstwhile knight of the road.

Now she would only have time for a quick shower and a hurried snack before she had to trek back into the city to Scott Electronics. She hated being rushed on study nights. She needed to feel very calm and in control when she confronted Scott. Her pride needed to greet him with the same cool composure that he was showing her.

She swore as the key jammed again in the lock. She really should get a locksmith in. In fact, there were several small handyman's jobs that she must get around to doing. The apartment building was a grand old lady, the reasonable rents reflecting the unfashionable shabbiness of the building which hovered on the fringes of a fashionable inner-city suburb.

Setting down her burdens, she tried again without success. A kick to the solid panels didn't help either. As a last resort she stomped down the hallway and knocked at the next apartment, pinning on a smile when the door swung open, allowing a waft of fragrant Chinese spices to surround her.

'Hi! Would you mind if I borrowed your key again? I can't get my——' Her words were swallowed in a gasp of shock.

Instead of the slightly myopic gaze of her stooping neighbour, Grace found herself begging a favour of bold black eyes and a pair of shoulders that needed no padding to emphasise their formidable width.

'What are you doing here?' she stuttered faintly.

''I live here.'

'But you can't! Mr Johnson does! Where is he?' Grace peered suspiciously around his bulk.

'You're not very observant, are you, Grace?' Scott Gregory murmured gently. 'He moved out days ago. The lease on this apartment has been on sale for months——'

'And you *bought* it?' Grace's voice nearly squeaked in horror.

'In a manner of speaking.'

Her blood roared in her eyes. 'I don't believe you. You couldn't have. Dammit, what have you done with Mr Johnson?' Grace's temper, already smouldering, flared as she pushed rudely past him to glare around the apartment. To her horror, the room was a tumble of unfamiliar furniture and half-emptied packing cases that seemed to bear out his incredible claim.

'You can't be moving in. You already have a house. "A lavish cliff-top residence",' she quoted sarcastically from the article he had sent her. 'You can't want to live here, in a run-down old apartment building——'

He cut smoothly across her incipient panic. 'Can't I? You do.'

'But I——' *Have to* was on the tip of her tongue, but she just managed to bite the words back. 'I...I like it here. I like the character, the...the...'

'Atmosphere?' he tendered helpfully. 'I know...that's what I like about it too.' He thrust his hands into the pocket of his faded jeans. In a black sweater with the sleeves pushed up to his elbows he looked more intimidating than he did in a suit, more—God forbid—sinfully attractive. After his impersonal attitude of the past weeks Grace was confused. Was she imagining the sultry message in those deep black eyes? 'What was that about borrowing a key?'

'I can't get mine to work,' Grace said absently, looking frantically around the room again, hoping that this was all some wretched, rain-induced illusion. 'Mr Johnson's key fitted my lock as well, with a little bit of manipulation. You haven't changed the lock, have you?' She looked at him with fresh dismay.

'Do you mean to tell me that you knew you had a faulty lock and didn't do anything about it?' Scott asked with ominous calm. 'Do you realise that if *his* key could be made to fit then so could someone else's? Someone you *don't* know. Someone who could walk in and out of your apartment at will and might even be there waiting for you now? A robber, or rapist, or worse——' He had worked himself from quiet menace into a thundering rage with a speed that took Grace completely by surprise.

'I thought rape *was* the worst fate for a woman,' she joked feebly. There was a blistering silence, during which Grace shifted uneasily, knowing his contempt was justified. 'I'll get the lock fixed tomorrow.'

'Tonight,' he corrected.

'It's too late.' Even if she could afford to pay the overtime, she wouldn't, on a point of principle. Scott might think he had free reign to bully her over her studies but he had no control over her private life.

He was not to be dismissed. 'It's never too late, Grace. I'll arrange it.'

'No, thank y——' Her dignified refusal was ruined by a sneeze. The narrowed black eyes suddenly dropped to scan over her limp clothes under the unbuttoned coat. He reached about to confirm the dampness with a brief touch and she leaped back as if he had pulled a gun. He withdrew his outstretched hand, his thickly arched brows rising at her skittishness. She sneezed again.

'You'd better get out of those wet clothes before you freeze to death.'

'I will, when I get into my apartment,' she said stonily. 'I'm already running late. I had car trouble.'

'Then it's a good thing you don't have to worry about using your car again tonight,' he said smoothly, pulling a set of keys out of his pocket and steering her out of the door.

'What do you mean?'

He unlocked her door with exquisite ease, giving her a look of searing condemnation as it swung open. He put a thick-muscled forearm across the doorway to stop her instinctive forward motion and preceded her into the apartment, checking all the rooms with swift efficiency before returning to the high-ceilinged living-room.

'I mean it's rather pointless for us both to drive all the way into town and back when we live within a few feet of each other. It would be much more sensible to save the time and expense of travelling and have to-night's session here.'

Grace's stomach tightened. Very sensible. So why did she suddenly feel trapped? 'In my apartment, you mean?'

'Or mine.'

'I think here would be better,' she said quickly.

He smiled, as if confirming a private thought. 'Fine. Have you eaten?'

He knew she hadn't. She had only just got home from work. 'I'm not very hungry,' she lied. 'I was just going to make an omelette or something...'

'Surely you need something more nourishing after a day like today, especially when you've been through a drenching. Why don't I bring over my lemon chicken and fried rice? Then we can eat and work at the same time. A sort of business dinner.'

Grace gave him such a look of quaint disbelief that his mouth quirked again, making her feel warm all over.

'I'm sure you only ordered enough for one——' she began, trying not to be defeated by his calm onslaught of reason.

'I'm cooking, and there's plenty.'

'*You're* cooking?' This time her disbelief was less flattering.

'I can do other things besides make money and tutor sulky students, Grace,' he said pointedly.

'I do not sulk!'

'Good. That's settled, then. You have a shower and get some dry clothes on and I'll bring the food over.'

'I want a bath,' she contradicted him automatically, trying to stem the tide of inevitability that was sweeping over her tired brain. It was a mistake. They both immediately pictured her lying in the bath, nude and soapy. Grace flushed and Scott's eyes glittered wickedly. No, she hadn't imagined it. He was back on the prowl again!

'Whatever turns you on, Grace.'

Before she could take issue with his provocative murmur he was gone, and she satisfied her fury by slamming the door viciously behind him. Then she had to open it again and bring her things inside. She lingered to put her chrysanthemums in a vase before she moved towards the bathroom. Let him cool his heels until *she* was ready. How dared he move in next door? She didn't for a moment believe that he was here because of the 'atmosphere'—any more than she was. But at least her reasons were straightforward. His were...his were...well, she feared to contemplate what they were. She turned on the bath taps. She didn't want a bath. She wanted the quick hot blast of a shower on her skin. But she was damned if she was going to let him manipulate her every move. It didn't occur to her, as she lay back in the bath fruitlessly trying to enjoy it, that by her over-reactions to his suggestions she was doing exactly that.

The bath certainly warmed her, but it didn't relax her. She was just wondering whether to wash her hair too when she heard a masculine voice near by. His key! Scott Gregory had used his key to let himself into her apartment. Of all the gall!

Grace nearly killed herself leaping out of the bath, skidding on the floor and knocking her elbow against the towel rail. She dried herself with a fury that made her skin tingle, threw on a dark blue angora cowl-necked sweater and cream trousers that were the first thing she grabbed out of her drawer, and stormed out into the lounge.

'Get out of my apartment or I'll call the cops, you——!'

The two men turned, one startled, one amused, at the barefoot virago, her normally glossy cap of hair a steamy, and steaming, black tangle around her embarrassed face.

'No need to go that far, Grace. In fact, James here works for Scott Security, so in a sense the cops are already here,' Scott told her with suspicious gravity. 'He's just put on a deadlock and chain for you and he'll be back tomorrow with a spy-hole for the door and an alarm and smoke-detector system. Thanks, James.'

The young man in the grey overalls took the hint and gathered his tools. 'My pleasure, Mr Gregory—ma'am.' He almost, but not quite, smirked as he withdrew.

'For goodness' sake, Scott, I don't need all that!' Grace hissed at him. 'This place may be old but it's not a crime-infested slum. There's nothing so valuable here that I have to protect it like Fort Knox——'

'That's purely a matter of opinion,' murmured Scott, unmoved by her resentment.

'I'm not going to pay for unauthorised work. If you send that man back I'll complain to the landlord——'

'Go ahead. Complain.' Scott folded his arms and cocked his head in a listening attitude.

Realisation dawned. 'You...you bought this entire *building*?' Grace choked.

'I told you, I liked its...' he looked her over from curling bare toes to steamy head and smiled '...atmosphere. Don't worry, Grace, this isn't a melodrama. I'm not going to toss you out in the snow if you don't let me have my wicked way.' He twirled an imaginary moustache.

'If you tried I'd sue you under the Tenant's Protection Act,' she told him icily, not showing one glimmer of amusement.

'Cold-hearted bitch,' he said softly, admiringly.

She felt a sizzle of ridiculous pride and frowned fiercely. 'You'd better believe it,' she threatened sternly.

'Oh, I do, I do,' he vowed. 'How about taking a bite out of my cooking instead of my vulnerable hide?' He moved over to the table and lifted a casserole cover invitingly.

Grace's nostrils twitched as they were enticed by the same mouth-watering aroma that had filled his apartment. If it tasted as good as it looked he had earned his right to his smugness. She moved reluctantly over to peer in at the plump, golden-yellow chicken sitting in its fragrant nest of fried rice. He had, she noticed, taken it upon himself to set the table with her best crockery and silver.

'I don't like you coming in here and making free with my things,' she said weakly.

He picked up a fork and scooped out a little of the rice and held it to her lips. 'Taste? I'm sorry, Grace, but James arrived and wanted to start work. I didn't think you'd appreciate having to trek out in a towel to deal with him. And I thought it would be a nice surprise for you to have everything ready when you got out of the bath. OK?'

Grace nodded, aware of his eyes on her mouth. The rice was superb. Then she wondered if he was asking whether she forgave him for coming into the apartment uninvited. He was dishing up now, looking so contentedly domestic that her acid remark of displeasure dissolved on her lips. It would seem petty to argue now, when he had gone to all this trouble... as long as he understood it couldn't happen again.

'Where did he put the keys to the deadlock?' she asked, and he gave her a faintly wounded look.

'In the kitchen. *Both* of them.'

'Good.'

When she saw that he hadn't put wine on the table, but iced water instead, she felt a little of her nervous tension drain away. With a clear head she would be equal to any of his cunning tricks.

She wasn't quite equal, though, to his charm. He talked about his trial and error method of learning to cook and the off-beat twosome who had comprised the moving company he had used. He asked her advice on local services and shops. She knew that she was being charmed, but she was helpless to prevent it.

'I don't understand you,' she uttered helplessly when
he had removed the chicken and astonished her anew
with a delectable chocolate mousse, also made by
himself.

'For which I'm grateful,' he murmured, thick lashes
screening his thoughts as he watched her enjoy the thick,
creamy dessert.

'You—you must have been cooking all afternoon,' she
said, feeling herself obscurely compromised more with
every delectable swallow.

'Evening,' he corrected her. 'It's only time-consuming
when you don't know how. When I was a child my
mother and I spent a lot of time in the kitchen. It was
the one place in the house that was always warm. My
mother believed that food should be treated as the mir-
aculous blessing it was. She taught me to cook as a kind
of celebration of the infinite diversity of life..'

As always when he mentioned his mother, his voice
sounded younger, less inflexibly cynical. Grace put down
her spoon. 'Why are you doing this?' she asked bluntly.

'Doing what?'

'Being...*nice*.'

He shrugged. 'Maybe I'm a nice man.'

'But you're not, everyone knows you're not!' she
blurted out. 'You must be after something!'

He didn't defend himself from the ringing accusation.
He leant over and dabbed a piece of chocolate from her
chin with his napkin and then lazily got to his feet and
sauntered over to her velvet couch, one of the few good
pieces she had salvaged from the sale of the house and
contents.

'Shall we get started?'

Grace looked from the couch to him, her thoughts in
her eyes and he shook his head chidingly.

'Work, Grace. Work. That's why I'm here, remember.'

'Oh, I remember all right,' she snapped, annoyed at being the victim of her over-awareness. 'I just wondered whether you did!'

'How about moving these flowers so I can spread out the books?' He indicated the vase on the coffee-table.

She saw that he had brought his briefcase with him, too. She picked up the flowers and placed them on the main table.

'They suit you in this mood.'

'I beg your pardon?' She turned around and regarded him loftily.

'Chrysanthemums.' He lazed back on the deep-cushioned couch. 'They always seem like such an insufferably bossy flower to me.'

'Oh, really!' Grace suddenly had an attack of severe suspicion. He was just a bit too amused. 'Was it you?'

'I beg your pardon?' he mimicked her haughtiness with a smile that mocked.

'Did you send me these?'

The smile died out of his eyes, although his mouth retained its thin curve. 'Aren't you asking the wrong man? Isn't Conway the one who sends you flowers?'

She had come this far. She might as well eliminate the scariest possibility. 'So it wasn't you?'

'You mean you really don't know?'

She was sure the slight change in his tone meant that he was being deliberately obtuse. 'Did you send them or not?'

'Do you often get flowers from persons unknown?' He answered her question with one of his own.

'All the time!' She lost patience with his evasiveness. 'Every Monday for the last four months, to be exact.'

'Are you serious? You mean you really don't know who's sending them to you?' He sat forward, his laziness dropping from him like a cloak. He then proceeded, with ruthless thoroughness, to drag from her the whole story of her secret admirer.

'Have you reported it to the police?'

Grace's mouth dropped open. 'The police? Why would I want to do that?'

'Because it might be some psycho, that's why. Someone with an unhealthy obsession. Have you had any strange phone calls in the last few months?'

'Only the usual wrong numbers...' Grace was stunned enough to reply. Such a vile explanation had never even occurred to her and she was furious with him for tainting her innocent enjoyment with his wild accusations. For it *was* a form of accusation, she realised. As if he was blaming her for being the recipient of an unsolicited compliment!

'How do you know they're wrong numbers?' he rapped out.

'Because they tell me—— Oh, for goodness' sake! You're the one with an unhealthy obsession——'

'What in the hell do you mean by that?' He rose abruptly to his feet, towering over her barefoot figure, seeming huge, and enraged all out of proportion to her comment.

'Nothing, nothing——' She tried to back away, holding up her hands, but he caught her upper arms in a punishing grip and held her tightly. She gasped, instinctively arching away from the densely packed muscles of his deep chest. 'I mean that only someone like you would turn a thoughtful gesture into some kind of perverted threat——'

'What do you mean, "someone like me"?' he snarled, leaning further into her, the heat and hostility pouring out of him like invisible waves of tension.

'You...you're always cynical about people's motives. You like to think the worst of them because it lets *you* feel superior. You're so...*calculated*—you'd never do anything as spontaneous as giving flowers and you can't understand someone who does. That would be too simple a gesture and you like to be an enigma, don't you, so that no one can get close? You deliberately put people on the defensive with your arrogance and your confrontational manner so you can manipulate them, so you can always be in control of everything and everyone, including yourself——!'

Once she had begun the words tumbled out faster and faster, impelled by the building awareness of her help-lessness. The only weapon she had against him was her tongue, so she used it cuttingly, hoping to slice through a chink in his cynical armour. Only as she spoke did she realise the real truth of her words.

With a jerk he hauled her still closer and for a moment she was genuinely afraid of the cold ferocity she read in his eyes, the deep and primitive need to hurt her that she sensed in the bunched muscles of his body. There was not a sound in the room except for their ragged breathing as they stared at each other, violence implicit in the air. But his response, when it came, was a shocking and inappropriate one. He laughed. A strange, hard, almost exultant sound that grated on her ears.

'Is this spontaneous enough for you, Grace?'

She didn't know what he was talking about until he moved his hips with a slow, sliding motion against hers, the defensive arch of her back providing the requisite pressure to make her aware of his sudden arousal. Lost in her anger, she hadn't realised that the clash of their bodies had been so intimate. Automatically she tried to arch even further away, twisting as she did so and tugging at his hands. The only effect was to intensify their mutual awareness of his hardness.

'God, yes, do that again,' he gritted, and Grace stilled instantly, raked with heat, as she watched him close his eyes and tilt his head back, exposing the strained tendons of his throat. 'Move like that again,' he urged her thickly.

'What do you think you're doing?' she spat at him, appalled at the weakness in her legs as he continued the grinding motion himself, releasing her arms to slide his hands over her hips, his fingers digging into her bottom as he held her tightly in position.

His eyelids flickered but remained closed, his thick eyebrows drawn together, his mouth parted to reveal his tightly clenched teeth. His whole body had hardened, rippling with a new kind of tension that was quite as violent as his former rage. He didn't answer her ragged question. He didn't have to. It was very obvious what he was doing. Grace braced her freed hands against his chest and pushed. It was like pushing against a steel wall. Except this wall was alive, shuddering and heaving with an intense internal pressure.

'I think you'd better let me go,' Grace whispered shakily, not caring any more if it sounded as if she was begging. She was. The slow, sensual undulations of his body were having a devastating effect on her own. Longings that she had thought buried with her husband were stirring, tiny thrills, thread-like tendrils began to shoot along her nerves, combining, splitting, recombining to form a thick web of smothering pleasure.

His answer was a faint groan, so indistinct and yet so utterly explicit that Grace nearly went under. She clung to his sweater, trembling, shocked and yet fascinated by his total passionate absorption. Although he still held her captive, it was Scott who was the prisoner. Grace realised now why he had to maintain such a tight conscious rein on his emotions: it was a matter of survival. Such a passionate nature must be at constant war with his intelligence. She looked at him with new and curious eyes. Grace had had no other lover but Jon, and Jon had been wonderful, but they had loved each other and he had always been tender and very concerned for her pleasure. Scott's sexuality was more primitive, more savage and intense, its very selfishness wildly flattering. He was openly aroused and enjoying it. He wasn't holding back in order for his partner to catch up with him, he was assuming that she would be just as frank and greedily uninhibited in demanding her share of the pleasure. For an instant Grace was tempted to test that assumption, to meet the reckless challenge. But then she remembered who and what she was and where they were, and fought the sinful impulse.

Unfortunately, before she could assert her fast-dwindling common sense, Scott had pre-empted her, pushing her away as suddenly as he had possessed her.

'Don't,' he told her hoarsely as her hands fluttered shakily in front of her, having lost their anchor of resistance. 'Don't move. Just stay well away from me.' He met her shell-shocked gaze with a slightly dazed one of his own.

His audacity was breathtaking. '*Me* stay away?' she said raggedly. '*I* wasn't the one who grabbed and...and...'

'Ravished?' A glimmer of humour showed, although his voice was still rough and choppy, his eyes still smouldering with the aftermath of his brief blaze of passion. 'No, but you goaded me into it...whether it was consciously or unconsciously. You wanted to see me lose my cool, so quit acting so outraged that I obliged.' His humour hardened into a more aggressive taunting. 'You enjoyed it, too, didn't you, Grace? You liked me shaking in my shoes to have you.'

It was such a startlingly vivid expression of sexual need that Grace could feel a fresh wave of heat sweep over her. She dropped her eyes so that he might not see the admission of guilt in them and found herself staring inadvertently at the physical evidence of his desire. She couldn't help a quick intake of breath, and pressed her hand to her newly tender breasts as her eyes whipped back up to the safety of his face. To her shock, he had followed her gaze. He was looking down at himself with a rueful amusement tinged with satisfaction that was both flattering and infuriating.

'There's no need to look so damned proud of yourself!' Grace snapped, forcing her hand back down to her side, remembering what a master Scott was at interpreting body language. There was certainly no doubt about what *his* body was saying...or, rather, screaming!

'No, you're right. I should be thoroughly ashamed of myself,' he agreed meekly, but his swagger as he moved back to the couch betrayed him. He sat down a trifle awkwardly, knees bent, legs splayed, and Grace flushed more furiously than ever. Unforgivably, he laughed. 'There's nothing I can do about it, Grace; I'm afraid it's an involuntary response. If we just ignore it, it'll go away of its own accord.'

'I think that *you* ought to go away,' she said firmly. 'I...don't feel like studying tonight.'

'You have a headache?' he guessed, still with that sly amusement. Then he seemed to take pity on her confusion. 'All right, Grace, no lectures tonight. But I'd like you to see something.' He opened his briefcase, ignoring his condition more successfully than Grace was able to, and took out a blue folder, shifting sideways on the couch to make room for her. 'Come here and look at this.'

He opened the folder and when she didn't move he looked up, and sighed. 'What do you want, Grace? A promise that I'm not going to leap all over you again? Very well, I promise. If the urge to be spontaneous comes over me again tonight I'll resist it...whatever the provocation. Now, what we have here is a breakdown of Blair Components' existing markets and the potential for expansion within the present framework of the company...'

As Grace listened she realised that he truly had switched his attention wholly to the matter in hand. His body might still be aware of her as a woman but his energy was now redirected towards a different kind of persuasion.

'I appreciate what you're trying to tell me, Scott, but Blair isn't in a position to expand at this time,' she protested when she had disciplined her own unruly emotions sufficiently to follow his reasoning.

'Not right now, but if and when this joint venture gets off the ground you'll find there's a natural spin-off in interest for Blair. The company has been stagnating for too long. There'll be opportunities for you to grab, and if you've already prepared the groundwork for them then you'll have a natural advantage over the opposition.'

'You can't expect me to make that kind of decision now,' Grace said, feeling a familiar rise of resentment at the implication that Jon hadn't been quite as good a businessman as he had appeared. 'Blair Components is a small company. Jon liked it that way. He didn't like the impersonality of huge corporations——'

'And are you going to always run your business, and your life, as Jon would have wanted you to? That pretty well narrows your options for the future, doesn't it, Grace? When are you going to start making independent decisions for yourself?'

'I am!' At his mention of Jon Grace felt her resistance stiffen. 'I know what I'm capable of coping with and it's certainly not the kind of expansion that you're advocating.'

'Not yet, I agree. But I think you underestimate your potential. If you decide that running this company is really what you want to do with the rest of your life then you'll eventually need the satisfaction of fresh challenges. I'm not suggesting any radical changes to start with. All I'm suggesting is that you begin thinking ahead...'

Grace forced herself to acknowledge the sense of his words. He was talking to her as one intelligent human being to another. There was no condescension in his tone, as there always had been in Jon's when he had told her not to worry her pretty head about finances. Evidently

Scott thought that her pretty head was more than capable of worrying. But thinking ahead made her feel confused and uneasy. The phrase that had snagged in her mind was 'if you decide that running this company is really what you want to do with the rest of your life...'

Was it? She had convinced herself after Jon died that taking over the company was her duty and her destiny. It was the lifeline that had hauled her out of a black pit of despair, but the desperation with which she had grasped it was now easing. Was she really tough enough to survive in the cut-throat environment that bred men like Scott Gregory? Did she want to become a business clone whose sole goal in life was to make another sale, another dollar?

Grace had never seriously contemplated having Jon's baby—she had flung that at Scott just to anger him—because she firmly believed that every child deserved to start out life with the security of two parents. But that instinctive desire for motherhood still yearned to be fulfilled. It was like a time-bomb ticking away inside her. It meant that she was vulnerable in a way that her male competitors and colleagues never were.

Was Scott really as helpful as he seemed, or was he intent on exploiting her feminine weaknesses for his own purposes?

'Why are you giving away a business advantage like this? What do you expect in exchange? Gratitude? Or something more tangible?'

Her accusation left him so unruffled that she decided to be more insultingly explicit. 'Is this some kind of bribe to get me to go to bed with you, now you live so *conveniently* next door...?'

'I won't be so easy to provoke this time, Grace,' he murmured evenly. 'We both know that when we make love it won't be a matter of bribery...just an impulse that neither of us can control.'

'Don't flatter yourself! I would never go to bed with a man just because of an *impulse*!' Grace jumped up, cringing inwardly at the thought that she was no more to him than that. 'Unlike you, I have some discrimination——'

'Are you implying that I live a promiscuous lifestyle?'

'I don't have to *imply*, it's the truth!'

'And that's the only objection you have to consummating this powerful attraction between us?'

'No, it's not, but it's a fairly important consideration in this dangerous age, wouldn't you say?' Grace said cuttingly, knowing that she was being the one provoked now and conscious of the possibility of a trap.

'Oh, very. I understand and applaud your caution...or should one call it *calculation*? That's why I thought it might be a good idea if I gave you this.' He withdrew his wallet from the back pocket of his jeans and extracted a folded sheet of headed paper. He unfolded it and held it out to Grace, who took it reluctantly, consciously arranging her face into an unreadable mask as she deciphered the scrawling hand.

She was glad she had when she finally realised what she was reading.

'What is this?' she asked with icy false calm.

'A clean bill of health from my doctor. Dated this week. So that gets rid of communicable disease as an excuse——'

'You——' She almost choked on her hectic embarrassment. 'You *asked* your doctor to write me this letter?'

'Don't worry, Grace, I wasn't indiscreet. I didn't mention your name. See, it isn't addressed to you personally——'

'"To whom it may concern". How very appropriately indiscriminate!' she raged. 'But it doesn't concern *me*.'

'Not even the little titbit at the end about how fertile I am?'

Grace knew she was now scarlet. He had even requested a sperm-count from the laboratory. She was mortified!

'That least of all!' She marched over to the door and threw it open. 'Now will you get out of my apartment or do I have to call someone to throw you out?'

'Who? Your secret admirer, too cowardly to lay his masculine pride on the line by pursuing you openly?' Scott sauntered past her, pausing to look deep into her angry eyes. 'I'm not afraid, Grace. I want you to know exactly who it is that wants you . . . badly enough to risk public humiliation and private failure. You have a great deal of power over me—are you woman enough to use it as it could be used, to benefit us both?'

Before she could reply he ran a warm finger across her parted lips. 'I'm also giving you notice that there'll be no more hiding behind our business relationship— for either of us. From now on, things are going to get very, very personal!'

CHAPTER SIX

GRACE was being wooed.

That was the only word that could adequately describe Scott's new tactics, she decided, although 'woo' perhaps wasn't *quite* the right word, because that implied that his intentions were honourable!

It was difficult to believe that anyone could explain business-management techniques in a way that made them sound sensuous, but Scott could, and did. There were no more strictly business sessions on neutral office turf, and Grace gave up trying to pin him down to a formal time and place. Inevitably he would just turn up on her doorstep on one of her free evenings, books in hand, and invite himself in. He wore casual clothes that made him look distractingly sexy and ignored her protests and feeble claims of other engagements, prowling her territory like a big cat, marking it out as his own, feeding her tantalising titbits about himself that she told herself she didn't want to know; like the fact that he enjoyed rock operas but not the real thing, that he disliked jogging, that he shared her love of science-fiction novels and dislike for the pretensions of a great deal of modern art. He was constantly bringing her samples of his delectable cooking or small, insignificant gifts that it would have been absurd to attach importance to by refusing. If he wasn't bringing things he was leaving them behind—cuff-links, a tie, a pen, a note vibrant with his slashing style—so that even when he wasn't there she never felt quite free of him.

Her determination might have been proof against his roughshod arrogance and calculated charm but his warmth was something else. Grace was both bewitched and bewildered by the apparent softening in him, even though she suspected that it, too, was part of his campaign to lure her into trusting him with more than just her education. Not for her the cool reserve and calm detachment with which he dealt with the rest of the world. With Grace he was different. Only with Grace. That was a dangerous enticement: to think that she was special to him rather than just a challenge he was determined to conquer. He also made her aware of the aching inside her, the yearning for closeness and comfort that she had been sublimating in work and study.

Arguing with him hadn't driven him away, nor ignoring him, nor losing her temper. He especially liked it when she did that. He liked taunting her indifference until he had exposed it for the lie that it was. Most disturbing of all was the way he chose to reward her for her each loss of control: by touching her. He would get her so ruffled and furious that she felt like hitting him and then he would stroke her arm, or her cheek, or tuck a glossy swath of hair behind her ear and suddenly she would be breathless, remembering the shocking feel of his helplessly aroused body against her, the way he had trembled and moaned with the pleasure she had innocently given him...

'Grace—it's good to see you along at another one of our functions. The Chamber of Commerce is glad that you seem to be taking as active an interest in our organisation as your husband always did.'

Grace shook the chairman's hand with less enthusiasm than he pumped hers with as she murmured her greeting. She knew the importance of belonging to local business organisations and showing the flag at social occasions like tonight's, but she also knew that it wasn't her that the chairman was really welcoming.

Sure enough, he continued affably, 'Since Scott is going to make the key-note speech tonight, I *was* going to put you both at the top table, but he's requested somewhere out of the limelight, so I've put you both with the Taiwanese delegation. Scott said you hope to be doing some business with them soon...'

Before Grace could object the chairman had swung away to greet someone else, taking it for granted that she would be delighted with the arrangements that had been made on her behalf. She moved reluctantly on into the hotel dining-room, her resigned blue gaze sweeping across the clustered groups of men and women without finding a satisfactory target.

He had done it again. Wherever she went these days it seemed that Scott had been there before her, preparing the ground, smoothing her way, subtly linking them together in people's minds. His timing was incredible. Every time she walked into a function like this he magically appeared at her elbow, so that even if they had arrived separately it was clear that they were together. Once might have been considered a fluke, twice had caused raised eyebrows, three times and they were an accepted item. Like it or not, she was now perceived to be under the invisible umbrella of her 'special relationship' with Scott Electronics and its intense, aggressive owner. What would have happened tonight if she had turned up with a partner of her own choice? she wondered. Presuming of course that any man existed who dared to risk asking her after Scott had tacitly staked his claim!

'Miss me?'

She stiffened at the warm presence at her back, trying to quell the delicious leap of anticipation it brought. 'I only wish I could,' she said haughtily, without turning around. 'You don't give me a chance.'

He moved up beside her, around in front of her, eyeing her plain, high-necked black crushed velvet dress with amusement as he shrugged. 'Blame the long arm of coincidence. Is the nun-like look supposed to repress any lustful male thoughts? I'm afraid it has the opposite effect. I was taught by nuns, you know, and none of them was as sensual as you look in that dress.'

'By nuns?' The very idea made her eyes widen and a smile tug at her firm mouth when she should have been frowning at him. Coincidence had nothing to do with the constant crossing of their paths and they both knew it.

'It didn't take,' he confirmed with a matching glint in his eye. 'But it was the best school my mother could afford at the time.'

'Your *mother*? But surely your father would have paid for——?' She curbed her unwary tongue but she had blurted out enough.

'My father?'

She wasn't going to be intimidated by that frostiness, not when he made such a point of thawing her own frigidity. 'Lincoln Redman of RedWing Industries.' The giant electronics corporation was Scott Electronics' leading competitor.

'Been investigating me, Grace?' he murmured cynically. 'Why didn't you just ask, if you were curious?'

'I'm not,' she lied thinly. 'But everyone else seems to think I am. They're eager to impress me with how much they know about my new ... *associate*.'

He ignored her angry emphasis. 'And how much do they know?'

She moved restlessly but knew better than to try to evade him in this mood. 'Not much. Only that you and your father never saw each other, and that when he died last year you weren't mentioned in his will. Your stepmother inherited the company——'

His smile was a mere baring of his teeth. 'His wife. Not my stepmother, his wife.' The correction was insulting in its precision. With a firm hand he guided her to one side, out of the incoming flow of arrivals. He held her wary eyes with his, challenging her to admit the curiosity she had sought to deny him.

'You want to know? I'll tell you: my father was a bully of the worst kind. If something wasn't done his way it was worth only his contempt. He also had an exceptional ability to hold a grudge. He wanted to marry my mother but she knew that she wasn't cut out for the kind of queen-consort role that he had in mind. When getting her pregnant didn't change her mind he told her that if she wouldn't marry him he would refuse to acknowledge or provide any financial support for her child. And that's exactly what happened. I never even met him until my mother died. Then I was supposed to be grateful, to accept his name and the fact that my mother was to blame for keeping me from my rightful inheritance. If he had offered me love in exchange I might have been fooled, but to him I was just another possession, a pawn to his king, symbol of his triumph over the only person who had dared to challenge his selfish ambition. When I came of age I took my mother's maiden name back and walked out. If he had left me anything in his will I wouldn't have taken it...'

Grace's heart ached with compassion even as she was appalled at the bitter rancour of his words. It was evident that he had loathed his father, and still did.

'You must have hated him for dying,' she said quietly. By doing so Lincoln Redman had rendered his son's hatred impotent.

His head jerked as if she had clipped him on the jaw. 'If I'd gone to his funeral I would have danced on his grave!' he snarled.

He hadn't answered her question, she noticed, although maybe he thought that he had. 'But you must feel cheated. You're left with all that unresolved bitterness and nowhere to focus it.'

'Oh, I have a focus, all right...'

His smile wasn't pleasant and suddenly the pieces of a puzzle fell into place. 'RedWing Industries,' she breathed. '*That's* why you've been taking over electronics companies, and offering preferential deals to anyone who has business with RedWing...Blair included. You're trying to take over your father's company...'

'Not take over. I told you, I don't want anything of his——'

'So you're not building an empire, then, you're just trying to destroy one——'

Her censure penetrated his bitter self-absorption, provoking a savage response. 'My mother died because she couldn't afford a life-saving operation. She couldn't *afford* to save her own life, because she was trying to build a better one for me. She asked him for money and he told her that she had made her bed and now she could lie on it...but he meant *die* on it.'

'She *told* you that...?' The burden on a helpless child must have been unbearable.

His savagery froze into icy bleakness. 'No—I found that out later, too late. So don't talk to me of destroying empires as if it was a crime against humanity—my father *had* no humanity——'

'And what about the people put out of work for the sake of your revenge? What about *their* lives and *their* families, their hopes and dreams? Are they any less victims than your mother was?'

'Dammit, Grace, don't try and make me feel guilty—it won't work,' he snarled. In his dinner-jacket and razor-pleated white shirt Scott looked like the epitome of the civilised male, but his eyes, his face and voice gave the lie to the veneer of sophistication. 'In these economic times every industry is going through rationalisation. It's inevitable that some jobs are lost when I take over an ailing company. But I'm not a fool. I don't cut off my nose to spite my face. I've never closed down a company that has the potential to turn a profit just because it would damage RedWing. In the long run I've probably *created* more jobs than I've sacrificed.'

'As a by-product of revenge, not through any positive intent...'

'I never claimed to be a saint, Grace.' His gravelly voice raked her tender heart with its weary irony. 'But I figure I've paid in advance for my sins. Not even for you am I going to pretend that it won't be the greatest thrill of my life to see RedWing reduced to an empty shell that I shall crack like an egg...'

'Thereby symbolically destroying your father. Be careful what you wish for, Scott; look what happened to Oedipus.' Remembering his earlier disproportionate reaction to a suggestion that he was obsessive, it was a dangerous remark, but Grace's concern for him was stronger than her fear. She knew too well what an emotional desert bitterness could create.

'Don't worry, Grace, my sins aren't quite that black,' he soothed her with a smile that held a twisted lack of humour. 'I'm a master of my fate, not victim to it. What I do, I do in the full knowledge of my motives and actions. And there's certainly no danger of me ever lusting after my father's widow.' He moved closer, his brooding black glare lightening, changing, challenging. 'The only woman I lust after to the point of ignoring custom and morality is you...'

She might have known that his serpentine tongue would twist the conversation to suit his own purpose. As a diversion the seductive murmur was masterly. She went weak.

'I wish you wouldn't say things like that.'

'Why? I thought you respected honesty. I'm being very honest with you tonight, Grace. Knowledge is power, remember? I've just made you the most powerful person on this earth where I'm concerned. You know things about me now that no one else does...not just what I am, but what I think and feel. I wonder if you will be as honest in return?'

Grace felt the familiar flutter of panic in her chest. 'Why can't you leave me alone?' she said shakily.

'Because you're too much alone already.' His voice gentled, enticed. 'It's not good for you.'

'And you are?' she asked sarcastically.

'I could be, if you'd let me.' His voice dropped further, deepening to an intimate murmur. 'You're too serious, too intense. You need to relax more. To let your hair down once in a while. You're letting the pressure get to you. There are stress lines appearing under those lovely eyes.' For one awful moment Grace thought he was going to trace them with his fingers, but he was only lifting his hand to adjust his tie.

'*I'm* too intense!' Grace flicked back her head, annoyed that she might have betrayed her skittish awareness of his every move. 'You're the one who's driven, who's never satisfied with what he's got. You're the passionate capitalist.'

'Passionate?' He tipped back his head and laughed, drawing eyes envious and slyly curious. Scott Gregory laughing whole-heartedly in public was a startling sight. 'I'm glad that you see me as a passionate man. Not many people do. It's my *dispassionate* side that is usually most admired and courted.'

Courted. Like 'wooed', the word was dangerously evocative.

That Scott's thoughts were running along the same track but on totally different lines became obvious when he jolted her by asking, 'Was Jon a passionate man? What made you fall in love with him? Did he admire and court you in the approved fashion?' When she stiffened he said softly, 'Fair exchange, Grace. I opened up about my past with you; why can't you reciprocate? Have you something to hide?'

'Of course not!' Grace was quick to respond defensively. For some perverse reason what would have been difficult to tell him in more intimate surroundings was safe to confess in public.

'Actually his courting wasn't approved of at all—not by my mother, anyway, who was the only family I had.' She smiled faintly at the memory of those heady days. 'Jon and I knew almost as soon as we met that marriage was for us...but if my mother had realised that Jon was serious about me she would have found some way of keeping us apart. So we met in secret and in the end we...we...eloped.'

'How very romantic.' To her surprise, there was no hint of cynicism in his tone, only a calm, assessing quality that was infinitely more disturbing. 'He rescued the princess from her lonely tower and offered her his kingdom. And no doubt your mother eventually forgave the prince for whisking you away to his palace of luxury?'

Grace looked down into her drink. There was cynicism there now but it didn't offend her. His assumption was only fair. Most mothers would have been delighted if their daughters had made such an eligible match.

'No. No, she never did,' she replied quietly, feeling a wrench for what might have been. Helen Randell had died begrudging Grace her happiness, making her feel that she had failed as a daughter by offering her loyalty to a man, taunting her that she was also failing as a wife by not giving her husband the children he so desired.

Scott moved, his body masking her from the rest of the room, ever the ruthless opportunist as he inserted a careful probe. 'Why not? Did she think he was too old for you?'

'No!' Her wry smile refuted the ridiculousness of the statement, revealing more about her love and respect for her husband than a dozen angrily defensive words. 'My mother wouldn't have approved of any man who took me away from my career. She started me modelling when

I was still a baby and devoted all her time to building up my portfolio. She was my manager and agent as well as my mother. By the time I was ten I was supporting us both. She was quite plain, you see, so she couldn't do it herself, but she was determined that I could have it all—the freedom, the glamour, the money, all the opportunities that she never had, or had lost when I was born...'

'She saw your birth as a loss rather than as a gain?'

Grace hesitated, then lifted her chin, remembering his own unapologetic confession of the unsavoury details of his past. 'She thought my father would marry her when she told him she was pregnant. But he said he was too young to sacrifice his freedom for the sake of a kid. So she sacrificed hers instead. She was brought up very strictly. It was a tough decision for her to keep me.' And she had made Grace aware of it from a very young age, aware of how much she owed her mother for her very life.

'But perhaps the wrong one.'

Grace drew a sharp breath as he voiced the disloyal thought that had haunted her for years. If Jon had not come along when he had Grace often wondered whether she would ever have developed the independence of spirit to reject her embittered mother's view of life in general and men in particular. But the old loyalty still held some sway. 'She loved me, in her way...'

'But not in the way a child needs to be loved—unconditionally for its own sake. Did you enjoy your childhood?'

It was such an odd and unexpected question that she answered wryly, without thought, 'I don't remember having one. I was so busy all the time: dancing and singing and deportment lessons and working. At high school all the girls I knew envied me getting to mix with all sorts of glamorous people and travel places and miss school——'

'And miss all the giggling girlish confidences and the usual innocent teenage social whirl while you coped with adult responsibilities in an adult world and yet had no real control over either, over anything in your life. You were a woman before you had a chance to be a girl.' The guess took no great leap of intuition on his part. The simple fact that she used the words 'all the girls I knew', rather than 'all my friends', was a dead giveaway. 'It can be soul-destroying to find yourself made an outsider in your own life, can't it, Grace? That feeling of not quite belonging to one world or the other, of having lost your essential innocence without having acquired the maturity of experience, of being trapped in the limbo of someone else's distorted perception of who you are...'

Grace looked at him in wonder. She had never put it into words herself, but that was exactly how she had felt. For the first time she felt an awareness of him that was purely mental, totally separate from the physical tension that existed between them.

Soul-destroying? Some people, she knew, didn't believe that Scott Gregory had such a thing as a soul—or, if he had, he had bargained it away to the devil long ago. It was one way to explain his apparent detachment from normal human emotions like tenderness and regret. But Grace heard both of those qualities in his voice. The prickles of intense curiosity that she had struggled to deny now spread into an uncontrollable rash. She could no more have stopped herself asking than she could have stopped breathing, 'Is that what happened to you?'

For a breathless moment she thought he was actually going to tell her, to resolve the puzzle of his personality, reveal the deepest, darkest, most seductive secrets of his life. But his habit of caution was too ingrained. She could almost feel his mental withdrawal as he shifted back on to the attack.

'No wonder Jon had such an impact on you. I suppose the need for secrecy made it even more exciting?'

To deny it would be foolish and untrue. 'It all happened so fast——'

'How fast?'

She could tell by the expression on his face that he wasn't going to accept an evasion. 'A few weeks...'

'I see...' His eyelids narrowed, concealing the leap of flame that flickered across the black eyes. 'So you are one of those people for whom love happens like a thunderstorm on a summer day—suddenly, unexpectedly, violently...'

Grace recoiled from the image of herself at the mercy of an uncontrollable nature. 'I'm sure it was just a once-in-a-lifetime kind of thing,' she said firmly.

His eyes were mere slivers of glittering black. 'Are you?'

The smoky murmur made her shift uneasily and glance around the room. To her dismay, they were still attracting a great deal of discreet interest. She quickly adjusted her cool mask of aloofness, but Scott was too perceptive.

'Does it really worry you?'

'What?'

'The speculation? It's inevitable, I'm afraid, but if you like I can do something about it...'

She shivered. He wasn't offering to leave her alone. But he could, and would, stop the people—and the talk—stone-dead if she indicated it bothered her. Such action on her behalf would only serve to confirm the current gossip.

'*No*! That is...' She looked away and said, rattled, 'It's indecent, what they're saying...they know I'm still in mourning...'

His heavy-lidded eyes narrowed, masking his cynically amused comprehension of her unease. 'What do they say to you, Grace?'

'Who?' She took a glass of wine from a passing tray, purely for something to do with her hands. Scott's

shoulder brushed hers as he leaned to do the same, saying
blandly,

'The women. The ones who suddenly want to be your
friends and share little confidences.'

Oh, he was shrewd, far too shrewd about the frailties
of the human spirit. While the men she met were skirting
her with respectful caution, warned off by Scott's obvious attentions, the women had apparently declared her
fair game. The disapproval among the more conservative matrons and former friends of Jon's was up-
setting enough. Far more embarrassing was the lascivious
approval that her presumed behaviour had gained in
some quarters!

'Nothing.' Her blush gave her away. She took a long
swallow of wine to ease her dry throat.

'Grace.' Her name was a sad reproach.

'Well, what do you think they say?' she snapped.

'Modesty forbids me.' He hid his grin behind the rim
of his glass but it shone like a beacon from his eyes.

'Modesty! You?' Grace poured a wealth of scorn into
her haughty look. 'Don't make me laugh!'

'Why? I love to see you warm with laughter. Now let's
see if I can guess...' He tilted his head and regarded her
flustered expression with cruel enjoyment. 'Could it be
that, while they feel morally obliged to warn you what
a heartless bastard I am, they also envy you having such
a notoriously elusive bachelor dangling on your string?
Do they beg to know how you bagged me and pester
you for all the delicious details of our sizzling affair?
Do they urge you to thoroughly enjoy yourself but make
sure you dump me before I dump you, because I deserve
to have the tables turned on me for once...?'

It was as if he had eavesdropped in the numerous
powder-rooms Grace had been accosted in over the past
couple of weeks. He had even adopted the right breathy
hint of scandalised delight.

'Or could it be that they think the whole thing is as big a yawn as I do?' she said repressively, banishing her blush with sheer effort of will.

He looked dutifully meek. 'I'm sorry if I'm boring you. I promise I'll try to be more exciting in future.' Grace felt faint at the prospect of a Scott Gregory devoted to being any more exciting than he already was. Her mind and body were already in raging conflict.

'I won't have an affair with you,' she said, driven to a crude, uncharacteristic bluntness.

'Why not?' he asked mildly.

To her horror, for a dizzying moment she couldn't come up with a good reason. 'Because...because people will talk——'

'People already do,' he pointed out. 'Thinking the worst is a useful crutch that gives the weak the illusion that they're superior. But those who really matter in your life, your *real* friends, will trust their knowledge of you, of your integrity——'

'And it's showing integrity for a widow to fall into bed with the first man who shows an interest after her husband's death?' she lashed out.

'Not fall; that implies a casualness that you're far too fastidious to allow. So am I. And we both know that I'm not the first man to approach you since Jon's death...there's your secret admirer and the man with the fur coat fetish, to name but two. But this is not about your being a widow, it's about your being a *woman*.' He studied her unconsciously wistful expression and chose his next words carefully. 'I'm not asking for anything that you're not legally and morally free to offer. You don't have to choose sides—Jon or me. I'm not asking for your love, or the personal loyalty that you obviously feel still belongs to your husband. We're both young and healthy, and strongly aware of each other. We have nothing to feel guilty about. What harm could there be in our sharing a physical celebration of the

preciousness of life and its all too fleeting pleasures . . .?'
He raised his glass and brushed it against the side of
hers, twisting it so that his warm fingers briefly touched
hers in a seductive caress. 'A toast to the glory of life,
Grace, and to our potentially exciting future . . .'

The universe was encompassed by a pair of midnight
eyes. Grace felt poised on the edge of a momentous discovery as she was drawn into their vast, dark mystery.
They might have been alone for all that she was aware
of her physical surroundings, and the sudden intrusion
of Neville's dogged complaint came as a shock, the
question within herself that Grace had felt on the verge
of answering slipping once more beyond her
comprehension.

'Counting your chickens, Gregory? I still think you're
trying to move too fast . . .'

To Grace's surprise, she was first to realise that Neville
had completely misunderstood the intimacy of the toast
he had overheard. Thank goodness he hadn't arrived a
few seconds earlier! If she hadn't been looking at Scott
she would have missed the uncharacteristic moment of
furious uncertainty before he readjusted his habitual cool
mask. He glanced at Grace as he made his reply to
Neville, catching her faintly ironic smile, and to her huge
gratification faint streaks of colour appeared on the
slashing cheekbones. Emboldened, she raised her eyebrows. Nothing to feel guilty about? She silently mocked
his discomfort, enjoying one of life's most definitely
fleeting pleasures—that of putting Scott Gregory to the
blush. He was embarrassed to be caught boldly trying
to talk her into his bed. He wasn't so sure of himself
after all. The knowledge was headily reassuring. Her
smile widened into deeply feminine satisfaction as she
listened to Neville reiterate some of the doubts his cautious mind had summoned to greet the threat of Scott's
sudden interest in Blair Components.

If he was asking for reassurance, Scott's firm answers offered it, although Grace knew that it wasn't the younger man's business acumen that Neville doubted, just his motives. In fact, Neville had grudgingly admired the innovative plan for the company which Scott had suggested to Grace, but his innate conservatism led him to temper his admiration with caution. He wasn't going to be rushed into anything and he was determined that Grace shouldn't either.

When Scott was called for a few brief words with the chairman before the guests were called to their tables, Neville seized his chance to say pointedly, 'I did offer to escort you tonight, Grace, but you said you were coming alone.'

'I did come alone.'

'Someone ought to tell Gregory that. He seems to think he has the monopoly on your attention.' He paused and then lowered his voice and said abruptly, 'If you're sleeping with him, Grace, be very, very careful. He's not like Jon. He could hurt you. He doesn't seem to care about convention, or what people think about him. And the way you're behaving now, his attitude seems to be rubbing off——'

Grace paled angrily, incredulous at the inappropriateness of his comment. 'I don't think this is the time or the place to discuss it,' she said tightly.

'There's never a right time and place these days,' he pointed out doggedly. 'You're pretty good at avoiding the whole subject. I just have to grab the opportunity where I can. I feel that as a friend I have the right to tell you that I think you're getting in over your head. You've always been very circumspect, but where Gregory is concerned you seem to have lost your sense of proportion. You're acting recklessly and that's not like you. You know how important appearances are to a woman in your position...'

Grace felt an impatient surge of defiance at the familiar reproach, however kindly meant. She was sick of people telling her how to act and look. Look happy, dear, look sad, look cheeky... the eternal chant from her childhood. It hadn't mattered what she had felt inside, whether she had felt tired or bored or angry or sick, as long as it didn't show on the outside.

Even with Jon, she thought with a pang, she had had to pretend. For his sake she had pretended to be perfectly content, as if a baby were only incidental to her happiness when she had longed even more than he to have a child of her own body to love and to nourish. Jon had hated to see her ill or upset. He was sensitive to the difference in their ages, expressing it in an eagerness to buy her ever more expensive presents, almost as if he was competing against himself for her attention. His failure to get her pregnant had affected him deeply, so that she had tried to spare him that added burden of her own feelings. Now he could no longer be hurt and she was tired of being stoic and understanding and dishonest with herself to spare other people's disappointment. It evidently didn't occur to Neville that his own behaviour was starkly inconsistent—on the one hand helping her to face up to the reality of Jon's death and establish herself as an independent woman, and on the other implying that she was letting him down by doing so!

She and Neville parted on uneasy terms and Grace brooded on his words all through the lavish dinner, charming the inscrutable Mr Chan and his delegation with her quiet poise and elusive abstraction. The food was delicious and the wine flowed generously. Grace was as abstemious as usual until she discovered that Scott was subtly authorising her intake with discreet signalling to the wine waiter behind her back. At any other time she might have overlooked his arrogance, since it coincided so perfectly with her own desires, but tonight she was in a mood to assert herself. Did Scott, too, think she was incapable of knowing what was best for herself?

It would serve him right if she got herself utterly stoned right under his nose, but Grace decided that his misguided paternalism deserved a more subtle revenge, one in which she could retain full dignity and control. When Scott departed to make his speech she went into action.

Scott's speech was witty and articulate but Grace made sure that she appeared not to be paying too close attention. Every time his glance drifted in the direction of their corner table Grace raised her glass to her lips and drank thirstily. He wasn't to know that she had bribed the same wine waiter to make sure the bottle he delivered in an ice-bucket to the table and flourishingly uncorked had its label discreetly covered with a napkin. When Scott returned to the table to enthusiastic applause the up-ended bottle in the ice-bucket at her elbow had mysteriously changed from sparkling grape juice to a hideously expensive vintage champagne. The Taiwanese with whom she was now demurely flirting were sticking conspicuously to their red wine, having spurned her offer to share the grape juice. They were far too polite to comment on her and the waiter's hanky-panky with the bottles.

The first thing that Grace did when Scott sat down again was to order 'another' bottle of champagne. The second was to excuse herself. She was suffering acute discomfort, thanks to her rapid ingestion of large quantities of liquid! As she hurried to the relief of the nearest rest-room she threw Scott a carefully glazed smile and a flagrantly smouldering look that made a muscle clench in his jaw.

While she was repairing the ravages of the evening at the lighted mirror in the rest-room she was joined by a woman she knew only slightly and who had the ill-timing to jokingly ask if Scott was as impressive in private as he was in public.

Grace dropped her lipstick back in her bag and snapped it shut.

'If you're asking what he's like in bed,' she said with reckless disregard for truth or consequences, 'he's pure thoroughbred stallion!' She sailed out of the room with malicious glee, leaving the woman open-mouthed with shock behind her. The worm had turned. It felt so good not to turn the other cheek to people's intrusive rudeness!

Back at the table, she found that Scott had cancelled her champagne and substituted Perrier water instead. She ignored it, calling the waiter over and ordering a large brandy and ginger-ale. While Scott chatted smoothly with their companions she disrupted his concentration by whispering increasingly outrageous asides in his ear, delicately slurring her consonants. Grace had never been drunk in her life, but she had seen enough of it in movies to know it was just a matter of loosening one's inhibitions. So she laughed generously at remarks that were only mildly amusing and chatted expansively, showing a marked enthusiasm for the kind of light-hearted flattery she usually disdained. She was subtle enough that a stranger wouldn't have noticed anything radically unusual in her behaviour, but Grace could feel Scott growing more and more tense at each fresh example of her uncharacteristic daring. Unfortunately, she had to drink the brandy, but its effect on her after the lavish meal was minimal compared with the giddy pleasure of taunting Scott.

She shifted her chair closer to his, ostensibly to talk across him but taking the opportunity to lean against him, steadying herself with a hand on his leg. The muscles were like granite under her fingers, his upper body going rigid as her hand began to slide apparently by accident towards his inner thigh. A tremor rippled through the hard muscles and his hand suddenly clamped down on hers under cover of the white linen tablecloth. She blinked at him with wide, hazy blue eyes.

'Something wrong, Scott?' she drawled innocently. 'You seem to be very stiff and starchy all of a sudden.'

The *double entendre* was unpremeditated, but, having inadvertently let it slip, she decided that she might as well be hung for a sheep as a lamb. She leaned further over him, the side of her breast pressing generously against the arm he had braced under the table.

'I think maybe it's the strain of all of this attention,' she confided to the smiling Chinese gentleman on his other side, safe in the knowledge that the speed and lowered tone of her speech was probably defeating his only adequate English. 'The poor lamb is a very shy person, you know. He over-compensates by acting like a ruthless swine all the time but he's really just uptight and insecure, aren't you, Scotty? Why don't you have a few drinks and relax like me——? Oh!'

Scott had hauled her to her feet, her hand still firmly clamped in his. 'What a splendid idea,' he said. 'If you'll excuse us, Mr Chan, Grace and I will relax together on the dance-floor.' Then, with an unsettling air of finality, he added, 'And may I say again that it was a great pleasure to talk with you and your colleagues on an informal basis tonight? I look forward to our next meeting in the very near future...'

Grace didn't get a chance to hear Mr Chan's similarly polished farewell. She was marched off to the small polished square of wood floor that was already crowded with couples and firmly thrust into motion by a very unamused partner!

CHAPTER SEVEN

'YOU'RE drunk!'

The accusation, issued through his teeth, was an outraged hiss. Scott's reaction was everything that Grace could have wished for... and more. She tried a little hiccup, and almost laughed at the thin set to his mouth. Why, he was looking positively prim!

'I'm happy,' she corrected him, leaning towards him, her inner amusement increasing as she felt his resistance. Scott was keeping a marked distance between their bodies, as if her imagined intoxication might be infectious, his leading hand actually pushing against hers, while the clasp at her waist was more of a brace.

'Don't you want me to be happy, Scotty?' She pouted at him, tilting her head back and looking at him with what she hoped was sultry invitation. She laughed, a bold, wicked sound that drew glances, while Scott himself stared stiffly over her head.

'For God's sake, Grace, control yourself,' he whispered tightly. Was he embarrassed by her uncharacteristic lack of inhibition? Oh, it was all right for the playboy tycoon to taunt *her* with his experience, to overset her poise with those sinfully dark looks and honeyed phrases, but turn the tables and he wasn't quite so poised himself!

Grace felt a delicious thrill of power at the knowledge that she had him off balance. She deliberately let herself go limp in his arms, and, when his grip relaxed in relief, quickly slipped under his guard, pressing the entire length of her body sinuously against him. Her tactics immediately threatened to backfire. Scott's coldly rigid body seemed to be generating an incredible amount of heat, swiftly melting her imagined detachment. She rested her cheek against his chest and willed away her trembling response even as she measured his by the wildly uneven thump of his heart.

'You'll regret this tomorrow,' he told her tightly, his hands tightening painfully on her waist. 'What in the hell did you drink all that champagne for? Do you *want* to make a total fool of yourself, jeopardise a deal with Chan——?'

'Rubbish. He thought I was as graceful as my name; he told me so,' Grace said airily, thinking that it was too late to regret her hasty revenge. She moved gracefully in his arms to prove it, brushing her breasts against his chest, hoping that the crushed velvet would hide the multitude of her sins. She had never been sinful before. Except for her elopement with Jon she had always been a dutiful daughter, just as she had later been a faithful wife. Now she was neither daughter nor wife. She was Grace Blair. Herself. A woman.

'You're the only one who thought I was out of line,' she drawled mockingly, too caught up in her reckless self-absorption to monitor his surfacing awareness. 'Chill out, Scott. If you can't fight it, you might as well lie back and enjoy it...' The thud of his heart had settled down to a swift, arrhythmic beat that set up a sympathetic vibration throughout her body from her scalp to the soles of her restless feet.

There was a small pause as he steered her pliant body around another couple. Then he tilted his head to look down at her. '*Chill out*?' Amusement leaked through his iron control. 'I never thought I'd hear street-slang from that elegant, business-lady mouth of yours...'

Grace moved dreamily against him, fully immersed in her fantasy role of *femme fatale*. She linked her arms around his back and arched slightly so that she could see his expression. 'But I'm not a lady tonight, Scott, I'm a woman,' she said huskily.

'Should I lie back and enjoy that too?' he enquired sardonically.

That conjured up such indecent images that for a moment Grace was shocked breathless. Her lips parted as she tried to say something sophisticated and utterly worldly in response. She couldn't think of a thing and for a moment she feared that she had lost the edge. She bit her lower lip and worried it with her tongue and suddenly he was the Puritan again, his voice rough with threat, as he gave her a small shake.

'Behave yourself, Grace. Stop being so damned provocative. One dance, that's all you get. Then I'm getting you out of here before you start leaping on to table-tops and doing the can-can!'

'What a killjoy you're turning out to be, Scotty.' To his fresh fury, she suddenly spun out of his arms and danced freely for a few moments before cutting mischievously in on another couple. Soon Scott was glaring murderously over the shoulder of a bottle-blonde while Grace languished in the sweaty grasp of a nervous young man who was very aware of the hovering black-eyed menace. When Scott cut back in a short time later Grace was relinquished with ill concealed relief.

'You're playing with fire, Grace,' Scott warned her grimly. This time he held her so captively close that she could feel the lines of his suit being imprinted on her velvet dress. She had the feeling that if he had been able to shackle both her wrists behind her back without attracting attention he would. He wanted to cage her, tame her, but tonight, surrounded by the security of a crowd, she was determined to be untamable!

'Mmmm, I know, and I feel so gloriously toasty and warm,' she murmured wickedly, waggling her fingers at a passing male grin.

Scott swore under his breath and tucked her flirtatious hand between their bodies, capturing the other before it could perform some similar impropriety, bringing it to his mouth to mask his aggression in the pretence of courtesy. She had been right about the shackling!

'You're drunk,' he repeated raggedly, more as if he was telling himself than her. She rather liked the hint of desperation. It was almost as satisfying as having him grovel.

She laughed, a sensuous cat-with-the-cream look of satisfaction on her face as she widened her sea-blue eyes and purred wickedly, 'But not incapable, dah-ling . . .'

She timed a deliberate mis-step as she spoke so that her leg slid caressingly between his as they turned. He almost stumbled as she lifted her knee, briefly applying the pivoting pressure of her slender thigh firmly to the juncture of his. Her provocation had an immediate effect and she drew back instantly, finally aware that her teasing had gone too far. But it was too late. Scott had reached the end of his tether.

Five minutes later she was belted roughly into the passenger-seat of her own car.

'I tell you I'm perfectly fit to drive!' she raged at the man who was sliding arrogantly behind the steering-wheel and inserting her keys into the ignition. 'I'm as sober as you are!'

'For your sake, I hope that's a lie, Grace,' Scott ground out savagely. 'But if it is true then maybe you've done me a favour. If you were teasing me deliberately I don't have to feel guilty for what I'm about to do.'

'Do?' Grace asked faintly as the car sprang into motion with far more power than she ever managed to coax from under the unimpressive bonnet.

'Did you think I would calmly trot away like an obedient lap-dog when you got tired of the game——?'

'I . . . I . . . didn't think——' she began to splutter.

'No? Just instinct, was it? Chain the beast, then rattle his cage until he howls——'

'Scott!'

He hadn't looked at her since they had got in the car, driving with a narrow-eyed concentration, but now he slipped a grim sideways glance at her shocked expression and what he saw there seem to ease—infinitesimally—his ferocious tension.

The wolfish twitch of his mouth wasn't reassuring. 'You did, didn't you? You really thought I'd let you get away with it. You didn't think I'd have the guts to drag you kicking and screaming out of there——'

Grace swallowed. She had definitely underestimated her victim.

'I wasn't kicking and screaming,' she protested weakly.

'Not on the outside maybe. But your haughty Queen of Sheba act never did cut any ice with me.

'Scared, Grace?' he jeered softly as she swallowed again, this time audibly. 'You should be.'

'What about your own car?' she began weakly, hoping that practicalities might prevail where argument hadn't.

'I'll pick it up tomorrow.'

She shut up. It was easier to plot when she didn't have to concentrate on parrying his verbal thrusts. Oh, whatever had made her think that she could best him at his own game? She wished she *were* drunk, but even that escape route was denied her.

She tried to quell her nervous feminine reaction with thoughts of a more practical, bracing nature. The drive would no doubt cool down that scorched male pride. When they got back to the apartment building she would placate him, contrive to convince him that it had all been a silly mistake. For all his threatening manner, she knew instinctively that he wouldn't use violence to enforce his will. He didn't have to... all he had to do to seduce her was to take her in his arms again! But once she had bolted her door on him she would be safe from her own wicked urges. He could rage and huff and puff all he liked but he wouldn't be able to get in. The irony was rather quaint. All the security locks that he had insisted she have installed on her doors and windows would ensure that her virtue remained unassailable—for tonight at least!

She had almost convinced herself that she had already outwitted him when she noticed the unfamiliarity of their route.

'This isn't the way home!'

He ignored her. The moving light thrown by the passing street-lights illuminated his shadowed expression. It was a hard mask of satisfaction.

'Dammit, Scott, where are you taking me?'

'I told you. Home.'

'This isn't where I live.'

'Not your home.' He turned into a steep, dark, curving drive. 'Mine.'

The driveway seemed to drop away directly into the deep black glitter of Auckland Harbour. The orange lights that followed the high, graceful arch of the Harbour Bridge seemed to hover almost directly over the point where the driveway disappeared. Grace's heart was in her mouth as the car swooped towards the sea, but when they reached the lower curve into oblivion security lights suddenly flicked on and she saw the brick-paved courtyard clearly for an instant before the car was swallowed by the lower level of the house.

The garage door closed automatically after them, and for a moment after Scott cut the engine the only sound in the softly lit enclosed space was the faint ringing echo of the metal door. Grace was irresistibly reminded of the metallic springing of a trap. One that she had baited herself.

'Scott——'

'Welcome home, Grace.' He leaned towards her and she flinched, but he was merely flicking open her seatbelt.

She couldn't see him smile but she could hear the sardonic amusement in his voice as he added, 'No, not here in the car. I'm not so crude as to take up your generous invitation without due ceremony and at least a few creature comforts.' He leaned even further, reaching across her to push open her door, this time dragging his arm deliberately against her rapidly rising breasts as he withdrew.

'Get out.'

'I——'

'I'd *prefer* to go inside, but I'm flexible,' he purred dangerously, pointedly placing her car keys out of reach in the inside pocket of his jacket. 'If you can't restrain your wild passion and don't mind a little discomfort I'm quite ready and willing to make love to you against the dashboard——'

She was up and out of the car with as much alacrity as her fumbling apprehension would allow. His mocking laugh as he followed suit had her searching for the door, but he was there before her, opening it with a flourish and a small bow.

'After you, my queen of haughty disdain...'

All the way up the narrow, spotlit staircase she was acutely aware of the movement of her hips and legs, the breathless difficulty in her chest and, most of all, the steady, inexorable masculine tread that stalked her. The room at the top of the stairs was shrouded in darkness, relieved by vague glimmering white shapes that made her gasp.

'Afraid of ghosts, too, Grace? What a timid little thing you're turning out to be...'

The murmured words smoked across the small area of vulnerable skin between her shoulder-blades, exposed by the discreet scoop of her gown, whispering across her sensitised nerves.

There was a faint click and the room sprang into light. The white shapes were sheets, draped over bulky objects. Even the floor was covered by a dark green tarpaulin, and the reason was obvious. The walls were stripped and primed, but had not yet had their first coat. The kitchen, Grace guessed from the positioning of the shrouded fittings. Scattered about were cans of paint and rolls of wallpaper, brushes soaking in paint and the odd ladder or two. The only ghosts here were those of the absent tradesmen. Still, Grace's heart continued to flutter with a deliciously disconcerting fear, an excited apprehension.

Without a word Scott took her elbow and ushered her impatiently through several more similarly dust-shrouded rooms with the unswerving instinct of a guided missile, not bothering to turn on any more lights. The place seemed huge, as silent and brooding as the explosively primed man beside her.

'You—you're redecorating!' Grace grabbed at the chance to divert him from his relentless intention.

He didn't answer and she continued nervously. 'I—is that why you moved out?' she asked, meaning 'in next to me'. With a mixture of chagrin and embarrassment she realised that he had merely let her *assume* that she had been the major reason for his shift of residence by offering others even less likely. Right now it would be a relief if there had been indeed some practical *innocent* purpose behind his new acquisition. She dug her heels into the tarpaulin. 'You wanted to be out of the way while the painting and papering was going on here?'

He let her resistance slow him but he didn't let his grip ease. He had already been taken by surprise once too often this night.

'Have you been feeling hunted, Grace?'

Her answer was in her uneasy sidelong look. He smiled secretively. 'Now you know how I felt this evening: like the helpless prey to your brazen huntress...' Grace flushed, her whole body heating at his words. She *had* been brazen, utterly so, and she had enjoyed it far too obviously to try to deny it now. He let her dwell on her folly for a moment before he murmured, 'The answer to your question is...' his slow smile drew out the suspense for a wickedly long second '...*perhaps*...'

His eyelids drooped, not quite hiding the predatory gleam that smouldered in the darkness. He was still very, very angry and he wanted her to know it.

'Certainly it turned out to be very—*convenient*...' His free hand came up under her other elbow and he stepped around to face her, forcing her backwards and into the realisation that while he had held her enmeshed with his equivocating words he had been slowly backing her to the wall.

'I'm no one's *convenience*,' she spat, determined not to let him see the effect his calculated menace was having on her already chaotic nervous system.

'You have to admit you qualify in one or two forms of the dictionary meaning, Grace,' he drawled, driven to torment her the way that she had tormented him. 'You're certainly suitable for my purposes and needs and you're close by...but no, I don't suppose you could be considered "easy to use"...'

The fear that had inhibited her flared into open temper at his overt mockery. 'If you think I'll let you——'

'Challenging me, Grace?' he interrupted softly, and watched her hesitate as she realised the certain consequences of goading him from her very vulnerable position.

'Actually,' he continued almost kindly, 'it's a little late for second thoughts. You've led me this far on your merry dance. Now it's time to pay the piper...' He dipped his head and to her tingling shock bit her gently on the side of her satiny throat. She reared back, but there was nowhere to go, no escape that didn't involve going through that broad-shouldered, lean-hipped wall of male arrogance!

'*I* led you! You're the one who practically kidnapped me——' She was appalled to hear the breathy lightness of her words when she had meant them to be firm, accusing...

'Mmm. Exciting, isn't it?' He bit the other side of her throat. 'Just think how thoroughly helpless you are right at this minute. You're in a strange house, while I know every nook and cranny. All the exits are deadlocked. Even if you ran, where would you run to? I'm a man. I'm stronger than you are...bigger, harder, faster. You can't get away, no matter how hard you try. I can do anything I want with you. And there's nothing you can do about it, except...'

'Except what?' The mouth skimming her throat was having as violent an effect as his taunting words, arousing the deeply buried desires that she had tried to deny. He was providing her with a list of ready-made excuses to surrender, without guilt....

'Except lie back and enjoy it!'

She felt the curve of his lips against her smooth skin, heard the amusement in the sensuous rumble. He was laughing at her! Flinging her own words back in her face! He wasn't content with merely seducing her. No, he wanted to humiliate her, too. Sudden panic struck and with a fierce surge of strength she shoved at his solid chest. To both their surprise, he staggered back, far enough for her to dart away. With a roaring curse he gave chase.

Grace's heart hammered as she scuttled from the safety of one muffled piece of furniture to the next. She froze, listening for the direction of his pursuit, but Scott had also stilled. He was out there somewhere, crouched and aware, listening, just as she was, waiting to pounce. Her skin prickled hotly and she could feel the blood pulsing heavily through her veins. Grace shivered with a strangely febrile excitement. She peeped around what appeared to be a small table and saw a graduation of the blackness. A doorway!

Taking a deep breath, she rose to a low crouch and ran for it. As she did so she felt a rush of air as close as a blow and a throaty growl. He had only just missed her! She couldn't help letting out a little scream as she abandoned stealth and bolted, darting breathlessly from room to darkened room.

Scott was never far behind and at first she was grateful that he didn't switch on the lights, the better to find her, but as his taunting laughter infiltrated the night she realised that he was revelling in the chase... and so was she! Her inner certainty that Scott would never physically hurt her, even in genuine rage, gave an added piquancy to the situation. She had challenged him in the most elemental way possible and he was responding in a way that was as different and exciting as he was.

The feminine panic which had precipitated her flight became a deliciously erotic terror as the teasing game of hide-and-seek continued. Sexual tension flourished in the shrouded silence like a living thing. He was no longer in a hurry to catch her, whispering silky-voiced threats into the night that curled her toes and dampened her palms, describing in sensual detail what was going to happen when he found her.

It didn't take Grace very long to break. When Scott suddenly went quiet her imagination ran riot. She pressed herself even more tightly against the reassuring solidarity of what appeared to be a sideboard and quavered, 'Scott?' There was no answer and she tried hard to sound convincingly calm. 'Scott, this is ridiculous. Why don't you turn on the light and we'll talk about it sensibly?' Sensible was the last thing she felt but she could stand the waiting no longer. The room was one that overlooked the harbour lights, but the illumination wasn't sufficient to pick out anything more than shadowy details.

Grace was just close enough to the edge of her self-control to try shameless grovelling. 'All right, so I acted foolishly this evening. Now you've got your revenge we're even—aren't we?'

Silence.

'All right, yes, I admit it!' she cried. 'I pretended to be drunk to tease you but I didn't do it because...because I expected you to respond.' And may God not strike her down for that awful lie! 'I wanted to annoy you, that's all. It was wrong of me. Childish. I'm sorry. You were so sure you knew all about me that I just wanted to show you that you were wrong. Scott? *Scott!*' Her placatory tone slipped badly. 'Dammit, stop it, Scott, this isn't funny any more!'

A soft chuckle floated out of the darkness. Grace was too disorientated to guess its direction. She whirled a full circle and said shakily, 'I'm not playing your stupid game any more, Scott, so you may as well come out. I won't try and run away again. I promise.'

Silence. She began to tremble, not from fear but from helpless desire. Dammit, why didn't he come out and finish what she had started back there at the hotel...?

There was a soft sound to her left, a tiny echoing click that acted like a trigger on her taut nerves, catapulting her automatically to the other wall of the room, where she backed hastily between two tented objects that provided her with a solid sense of security.

A false sense, she discovered when a hand suddenly whipped across her mouth from behind, smothering her scream.

'So much for your promises, Grace,' came the clipped murmur in her ear. 'That was only my cuff-link. You ran straight into my arms.'

The hand across her mouth tightened as she tried to protest, and an arm lashed around her waist, drawing her back against a hard, familiar body. He hadn't lied in his silken whispers. He was as aroused as she by their

foolish game. She lay there for a moment, her head
against his shoulder, trembling and breathless. She tried
to speak and tasted the male fragrance of his palm. Instead of dropping his hand he trailed it deliberately across
her lips, his fingers curving into her parted mouth,
stroking the inner surface of her mouth and fondling her
tongue with an intimacy that was far more shocking than
any explicit sexual caress.

Her heart thundered in her breast as he softly probed
her moistness, stealing the breath from her lungs, as he
whispered, 'Do you like this, Grace? Your mouth is like
wet satin, wrapping my fingers. Use your tongue, suckle
me, tell me if you like the taste of me...'

The sheer intoxication of his husky plea made her
moan and he quickly let his hand drop. 'Am I hurting
you?'

She couldn't answer and his hand continued to fall,
until it settled on the firm roundness of her left breast,
his palm cupping her, feeling the pounding tumult within.

'You...frightened me,' she managed to say, her tastebuds tingling with each word, drowning in the full
flavour of him.

'This isn't fright, Grace...' His hand tightened and
then released, to flatten and move against her in soft
rotation, compressing the flesh in a way that made her
tremble even more. 'This is excitement. You wanted to
be caught, didn't you? You're as curious about me as I
am about you, only you wouldn't let yourself admit it.
Tell me now if this is not what you want, Grace, because
from here on in I can't guarantee my control...'

As he issued his rough command his hand moved to
explore her other breast, while his hard thighs straddled
her buttocks. The hand around her waist strayed, fingers
splaying wide against her velvet belly, digging into her
softness, reaching for the ache that was forming in the
pit of her stomach. His mouth was moving against her
shining cap of hair, seeking the sensitive hollows at the

nape of her neck. He was shaking, she realised with a
blossoming sense of rightness—just like that other time
in her apartment. He was handing control to her because she made him feel wildly *out* of control. She had
never driven a man so wild with desire that he didn't
know what he was doing...

'Scott——'

'God, don't say no, Grace. Not now.' He spun her
tightly in his arms and she made a discovery that
drenched her with sensuous delight.

'Your clothes...' He had taken off his jacket and tie
some time during his dark pursuit and unbuttoned his
shirt so that it hung free from his broad shoulders. The
hands that she had placed against his chest met with
bare skin—hot, damp, satiny skin covered with thick,
soft hair. His heart was almost leaping from his chest
and he shuddered as she pressed her palm harder against
him, marvelling at the strength and power rippling beneath the skin.

'I got hot, chasing you,' he said jerkily. 'I still am.
Wanting you makes me that way. Hot and so ready that
I can hardly stand.' He made a subtle movement with
his hips and groaned as he brushed against the thick
velvet folds of her skirt. She felt a fresh moisture break
out on his skin and in an instinctive gesture of ac-
ceptance leaned forward to nuzzle it from his chest, her
mouth inadvertently brushing against one of his large,
flat nipples in his nest of hair.

He made a choking sound in his throat, arching back
to give her free access to his upper body and in the
process ground his swollen hardness against the juncture
of her thighs.

'Yes, oh, yes, honey, do it——'

Grace barely heard his ragged plea. Scott was so exquisitely responsive to every tiny movement she made,
even to the very breath from her lips upon his skin, that
she was soon deep in the toils of a dreamy delirium. She

wasn't aware of the rip he made in the back of her dress when his shaking hands wrenched the zip down, only of the molten sensuality of his gaze as he steered her into a shaft of light near the window and studied her breasts, nestled in their cups of pure white lace.

'Sweet…pretty…did you wear this for me?' he asked thickly, roughly tracing the outline of the lace across the curving swells. 'Did you want me to take off your dress tonight, Grace? To admire you like this?'

'I…' His arousal was so flatteringly intense that she couldn't deny him the truth. 'Yes…' She closed her eyes, gasping as she felt the stroke of his thumbs across the seams, finding the rigid tips that were evidence of her own desire. He made a sound and she felt him kneel to pull her velvet gown over her hips, revealing the white bikini panties and suspender belt in the same simple lace design as the bra, demure yet sexy in their essential femininity. He made another sound, this time deep and guttural, his hands running up the backs of her thighs, pulling them closer, parting them…

She opened her eyes, clutching at his naked shoulders as he moved his mouth hotly against the lacy front panel of her panties and pressed a string of kisses from the soft pale skin at the tops of her stockings to the deep, frantic pulse at the hollow of her hip. The sight of his dark head moving against her and the sensations he was creating made her cry out in helpless wonder and he looked up, a dark flush crossing his face when he saw her starlit expression.

He stood and kissed her on the mouth until they were both breathless. Then, still holding her, he reached behind him, dragging the sheet off the nearest object. It was a smooth, polished mahogany dining table, its dark surface reflecting the muted lights from the sea. Grace imagined him laying her down on that smooth hardness and leaning over her, felt the melting pleasure of his touch. He turned her, pressing her hips against the carved mahogany edge.

'I've never made love on a table before,' she whispered raggedly, hoping that she wouldn't disappoint him with her relative inexperience. No doubt he was used to women who were terribly adventurous and sexually sophisticated. She thrust the jealous thought away and linked her arms around his neck, reminding herself that *she* could make him shake with passionate need. She could make up with enthusiasm for what she lacked in experience and he would never know the difference!

He stilled and she was afraid that she had destroyed the moment with her naïve little confidence. He lifted his head and looked at the table behind her. Then he stooped and swept her off her feet, but instead of tipping her on to her back his strong arms lifted her tight against his chest.

'No, not here,' he said hoarsely. 'The first time should be in a bed...' He began to move with Grace in his arms and she turned her hot face against his broad chest, adoring him for caring enough to make this exactly right for them, made to feel small and feminine by the ease with which he carried her.

'I don't want to wait.' She told him shyly of her need and his arms tightened, the muscles of his shoulders and neck bunching into prominence as his stride quickened.

'You won't have to.' He turned into another doorway, dipping an elbow against the wall until twin lamps glowed, their light filtered into a soft, golden delicacy by the cloths that swathed them. Scott didn't let her go as he removed the covering over the bed and stripped back the dark feather quilt. When he finally put her down it was on to crisp white sheets that released a lavender fragrance to mingle with the heated scent of arousal that perfumed their bodies.

Scott stood by the bedside, looking down at her. Then he spread his hands, revealing the fine tremors there.

'Look what you do to me. You make me weak.'

Grace reached out a hand and touched his ridged stomach. 'You're the strongest man I know,' she said softly, feeling the shift and clench of muscle under her fingers as she stroked them down to his belt. She tugged at it. 'I want you.'

The knowledge flared in his hungry eyes, hardening the planes and angles of his face until it looked as rigid as his body under her exploring hand. He caught her wrist before she would have touched him intimately, folding her arm back into the pillow behind her head as he knelt beside her. 'Say it again. Say my name.'

'I want you to make love to me, Scott Gregory.' Her words were a promise to give him all that he wanted, and more...

'No more running?'

She shook her head, unable to speak as he unclipped the front fastening of her bra, sensing that he wanted her to lie quiescently as he bared the last secrets of her body. She felt shy, like a precious gift being gloatingly unwrapped, but she didn't resent his moment of purely masculine triumph. The glory of the moment was also hers, this beautiful man hers. He was giving himself to her and asking nothing but what she was willing to give in return. For tonight and perhaps for many nights to come she would let him satisfy the hunger in her soul, colour the cold grey corners of her world with a warmth and vibrant life that would dispel, at least for a time, the loneliness she had come to accept as her present destiny.

'I want you, too. More than you can know. I hope I won't hurt you...'

Grace dismissed the odd remark along with all her other doubts as she welcomed the joy of loving again. Scott undressed himself with a fumbling haste that she found inexpressibly exciting and when he came down on to her she gasped at the violent energy of his enthusiasm.

What followed was like being ravished by a whirlwind!

The controlled, disciplined man had vanished completely. In his place was a greedy, intemperate, ardent and impetuous male, urgently intent on plundering each and every lavish pleasure of the flesh. Relax and enjoy was about all Grace was capable of doing as his sensual onslaught built towards a fiery climax. He devoured her, feasting on her body with blind hunger, biting lushly into her soft skin, sipping and suckling the sweetness from her achingly swollen breasts as his hands adjusted her body around his, moaning and shuddering so violently when she even lightly caressed him that she resorted to merely riding the exquisite storm.

The moment when he took her would live vividly in her memory forever. The shocking reality of his first thrust stilled them both. He lay, his chest shaking, half across her body, his head buried in the curve of her neck. Surely he wasn't going to stop now, thought Grace hysterically as her body slowly adjusted to the agonising fullness, and she felt the involuntary ripples of tension begin to absorb him even more deeply into her being. She plunged a hand into his sweat-drenched hair, and pulled his head back.

'Scott——'

She hardly recognised him. His mouth was full, reddened, the skin drawn tightly over the bones of his face, giving him a lean, hollow-cheeked wildness, the deep-set eyes open but blank with an inner turbulence. He looked almost totally insensate. Grace felt shaken by a sudden wave of tenderness, her fingers curling tightly into his silky-damp hair.

'Scott...' The tenderness flooded her being and was just as swiftly followed by another wave of intense feeling as Scott stiffened and pulled back slightly, the pupils of his eyes contracting, his jaw clenching as he fought the blind instinct that was relentlessly driving him.

'I'm hurting you,' he gritted. 'I went too fast for you... I'm sorry.' He moved up on his braced arms and tried to withdraw further but she stopped him, almost sobbing.

'No... oh, no——'

He hesitated and she moaned again, this time a bitter protest, 'No, please, no, not yet...'

She was fighting now too, and he watched, puzzled and then fascinated, as she moaned, her eyes wide with a strange fear and confusion. Her fingers slid laxly out of his hair to clench and unclench helplessly on the pillow. A deep rosy flush spread up from her damp, heaving breasts to mantle her throat and face. He realised then what was happening to her and waited, afraid to move again for fear of breaking the wondrous spell, watching hotly as the inexorable momentum built swiftly to flashpoint. Only when she rolled her flushed cheek sideways into the pillow did he move, cupping her face with his strong hand, forcing her to look at him.

'No, let me see... let me watch it happen to you... I want to know...'

Her eyelids fluttered at his husky command, her blush deepened, but she was too enraptured to feel embarrassed, too stunned by the speed of it all to deny him anything he asked. Her mouth trembled and parted and she began to gasp in light, shallow breaths that made her flushed breasts quiver deliciously, invitingly... He bent and touched a stiff pink nipple experimentally with his mouth, very gently. She jerked and cried out, exploding beneath him in a series of violent convulsions that almost unseated him. He gripped her thighs and held her steady while she sobbed and moaned and poured herself into him, and then, as she melted lovingly around him he at last began to move, uncertainly echoing her undulating movements until he established his own powerful rhythm, this time driving her with him, until

his raw shout of exuberant satisfaction signalled that the
whirlwind was spent.

In the morning Grace was grateful for the resilience
of her relative youth. Even after a long hot shower, her
muscles ached with the extravagance of her strenuous
exercise. She felt as if she had been battered, not by one
whirlwind, but several. And she had. If she had thought
that Scott's incandescent passion would swiftly burn
them both out she discovered, through the ravishing
reaches of the night, that she was marvellously mistaken. His desire, like his curiosity about her body, had
proved insatiable. And, although the second and third
time they made love it was not with the stunning speed
of the first, it was still fiercely, gloriously energetic. He
encouraged a boldness in Grace that she hadn't known
she possessed. He made her feel unutterably sexy, as if
she was the only woman in the world who could satisfy
his lavish appetite for lovemaking, and he devoted and
demanded the same kind of single-minded commitment
to creating pleasure that he did to his more worldly ob-
jectives. In short, he was every bit the fantastic lover
she had falsely boasted of. Grace smiled to herself as
she sipped her coffee. Was this a case of being hoist by
her own petard? If so, everyone should have such a virile
executioner!

'You look quite disgustingly smug.'

Scott had showered, brought her coffee and toast in
bed and casually dressed in front of her with the ease
of a man who was thoroughly satisfied with himself and
the world in general.

'You're looking fairly smug yourself,' she answered
boldly.

'Making love in the morning obviously suits us
both...and in the evening, and at night. By the way,
what are you doing at lunchtime?'

Grace couldn't help blushing. She wasn't *that* bold—
yet. If she and Scott were lovers for long she didn't doubt

that she could become very, very brazen. 'Eating,' she said repressively.

Scott refused to be repressed. 'Wicked, decadent woman.' He leaned over and tugged the sheet that was tucked over her breasts down to her waist. Grace squeaked and held out her cup, afraid she would spill some of the hot liquid as he bent to lightly kiss her rosy softness. 'Is all of you on the menu, or just selected divine parts?'

'You're a glutton!' Grace murmured weakly, closing her eyes, shivering at the tingling pleasure his delicately teasing tongue evoked.

'Ouch!' The coffee had splashed on to his cheek.

'Serves you right.' She didn't pull up the sheet, sitting primly among the crumbs and cotton sheets, deliciously aware of the contrast between her nudity and his dark, formal suit as he moved away. He had told her he had an early meeting—one reason for the necessity to rouse her just after dawn by making love to her sleepy, languorous body. Waking up to find Scott inside her was just one of the new, fresh pleasures of life!

'Will you meet me for lunch? This meeting should be over by then.' He straightened his tie in front of the mirror then walked back to her.

'If you want to...'

He cupped her chin, reminding her of the way he had refused to allow her to hide from him last night. 'I want. Make no mistake about that, Grace. I have no regrets. None.'

'Good.' She lifted her chin and tried for a little of the sophistication he was no doubt used to. 'I wouldn't like to think that I had disappointed you.'

To her annoyance, he laughed. He straightened, letting his fingers trail down her throat. 'There wasn't much chance of that, believe me.'

'Oh, are you so confident of your prowess?' she snapped defensively, feeling suddenly restless and argumentative. 'You can turn any woman into your personal love machine?'

He seemed unruffled by her irritable crudity, a strange smile still playing around his lips. 'On the contrary. I'm afraid I have no basis for comparison.'

'What?' Grace stared at him blankly.

He scooped up a slice of toast and bit into it. 'Couldn't you tell, Grace? Was my gift such a paltry thing? I thought one's partner could always tell.'

What was he talking about? To her horror, Grace suddenly realised that, although he had used protection afterwards, that first, rough coming-together had been utterly spontaneous and Scott certainly hadn't held back. She remembered that embarrassing letter from his doctor and blanched. Did he really think he was that fertile? That she might already be pregnant? How dared he find that so amusing?

'What gift? T-tell—what?' she stammered, raising her cup to hide the quiver of her mouth, hoping he wasn't going to prove as selfishly arrogant as she suspected!

'Why, that it was my first time, of course.' And, as she continued to stare at him uncomprehendingly over the top of the cup, his smile gentled into a tender warmth.

'You were my initiation, Grace. I gave you my virginity; you gave me my manhood.'

And, leaving her gasping and choking with shocked disbelief, a pool of hot coffee soaking into the sheets around her, he calmly turned and walked out of the house.

CHAPTER EIGHT

'*I THOUGHT one's partner could always tell... it was my first time...*'

Grace stared across the crowded restaurant, totally unaware of the chatter and bustle going on around her as she watched the man come in through the rain-streaked glass doors and speak to the hostess.

It was a joke, it *had* to be! Either that, or he had intended it as a distraction from any guilt she might start to feel about giving herself to someone other than Jon. If so, tasteless as it had been, it had worked admirably!

'*I have no basis for comparison...*'

Impossible! Grace shook the thought out of her head. Scott Gregory was twenty-nine, for goodness' sake! He had had women by the bucketful!

Grace saw the man at the door turn and look out into the room as he took off his damp coat. She remembered regretfully watching him don that dark suit earlier that day, piece by elegant piece, a slow striptease in reverse. Under that cool reserve was an extremely sensual, highly sexed man. He had demonstrated no strong religious or moral objection towards extramarital sex—quite the reverse where Grace was concerned! So his claim of complete celibacy was obviously nonsense.

'*I gave you my virginity...*'

She had sensed the sensuality in his nature from the moment they were first introduced... the heat beneath the ice. This morning's bombshell had to be a perverse example of that unpredictable sense of humour. Well, she wasn't laughing!

'*You gave me my manhood...*'

Why was she even entertaining the thought that he might have been serious? Warmth suffused her as she watched Scott exchange another laughing word with the hostess before he started across the room towards her. She was remembering his uncontrollable shaking, his rough eagerness, his constant whispering...'*Do you like this*...?' '*Can I do this*...?' '*Should I touch you here*...?' His frank groans of pleasure...'*Oh, yes, yes, Grace, do that again, it feels so unbelievably good*...' She had thought that his heated murmurs were his sophisticated technique of heightening their mutual excitement. But were they in fact the involuntary cries of a man who was experiencing those overwhelming physical sensations for the first time in his life?

No!

He was looking directly at her now, the black eyes fixed gravely on hers as he approached, ignoring the casual greetings of several other diners. His dark head glistened with a crown of raindrops. His direct look was a challenge, his stride a controlled, purposeful prowl.

She quickly picked up the menu and lowered her eyes to study it as he came to a stop in front of her. He stood there for a few moments in silence and Grace felt her fragile poise cracking.

She knew that she looked good, although it was sheerly accidental. She had driven home in a daze and and chosen the first dress in her wardrobe to wear in to work, a singularly inappropriate cream wool crêpe. The emphasis on her breasts and the soft, flowing lines made her look more like a frivolous lady of leisure than a hardworking businesswoman. Or perhaps she looked exactly what she was: a young and virile man's mistress! Grace could feel the colour begin to creep into her cheeks. Even when she was ignoring him he made her aware of her body...

No doubt Scott was thinking that she had worn the dress just for him. To appeal to her lover. Her sexy,

sophisticated man of the world. The one who was famed
for his emotional detachment, with whom she had
thought it safe to have a fling because there would be
no wretched emotional mess afterwards, no bitter sense
of loss to add to the burden of past grief. They would
both just calmly walk away with their hearts intact!

'Don't I even deserve a greeting?'

Grace's eyes jerked to his. They were wryly amused
rather than mocking or triumphant, as if he appreciated
her awkward dilemma and was as unsure as she of their
ground.

'*Was my gift such a paltry thing*?'

'Hello, Scott.' Instead of sounding crisp and decisive,
her voice was as thin and nervous as a girl's.

'Grace.' How could a single word say so many things?
He sat down beside her, rather than opposite, and leaned
to look at her menu. 'I'm sorry I'm a few minutes late.
Have you decided what you want?'

Grace's eyes flickered sideways and he was waiting for
her, his voice dipping to a husky drawl. 'Besides me, of
course...'

The ground firmed beneath her feet. He might not
realise it but his teasing provocation was much easier for
her to handle than his gravity.

'I can't stay long——' she began repressively.

'So you told my secretary. Fortunately I had warned
her not to accept any excuses,' he said drily.

'I happened to be very busy this morning.' Grace retreated to stand on her dignity.

'Doing what?' He leaned back in his chair, not taking
his eyes off her flushed face as he lifted a casually im-
perious hand in a signal for a waiter.

Nothing, of course. She had been too busy turning
his words over and over in her mind, searching for deep
hidden meanings that would render them harmless.

'None of your business.'

Unfortunately he seemed to understand her sullen retort perfectly. 'Me too. Mind-blowing, isn't it?'

Grace couldn't think of a better word that described his effect on her but his bland expression made her wary. 'What is?'

'Us. Together. Steak. Thick. Rare. I'm ravenous.'

For a moment Grace thought that he was comparing their carnal activities to the carnivorous pleasures of a juicy prime-beef fillet and then she realised he was selecting from the menu. The waiter looked expectantly at her and she hastily selected an item at random. When he departed there was a moment of heavy silence.

'Well?'

'Well, what?' Grace said innocently, looking anywhere but at him.

'Aren't you going to ask me?'

'Ask you what?' she said stubbornly.

He sighed and changed tack. 'Regrets already, Grace?'

'Of course not!'

'Then why are you afraid to look at me?'

'I'm not!' Pride alone enabled her to stare him in the eye.

'It's a little awkward for me too,' he said quietly. 'I'm not exactly sure what you expect of me, Grace.'

'What I expect?' She was startled out of her confusion.

'From our relationship.' That dangerous gravity again. He picked up her hand, which was lying clenched on the table, and held it despite her instinctive flinch. 'Don't tell me you don't have expectations, Grace. If I know what they are I would have a much better chance of meeting them.'

Grace felt the warmth of her blush spread throughout her entire body. He had certainly met all her expectations last night!

Scott began to smile again, his eyes glinting with masculine satisfaction as he murmured reprovingly, 'Other than the purely physical, of course—I know we have no problems on that score... I knew you were attracted to me, of course, but I wasn't sure until last night that you wanted me as desperately as I wanted you. Now I am. So don't even think of trying to dismiss this as a one-night stand, Grace——'

'I wasn't,' she denied truthfully. She was wary, bewildered and apprehensive, but the sweetness of his passion had been utterly addictive. After just one taste she knew that she had to have more...

His dark eyes smouldered. 'I'm not ashamed of people knowing that I'm your lover, but I'm cognisant of the trust involved.' His fingers were moving against hers and she realised that his thumb was moving back and forth across the twin bands of her wedding and eternity rings. For once she didn't associate them with the emptiness of loss. 'I won't lie but I won't embarrass you by emphasising it, if that's what's worrying you. We'll just take things as they come...'

His thoughtfulness was almost more than she could bear.

'It—it was just silliness this morning, wasn't it?' she blurted out desperately. 'I mean, you just said it for sheer shock-amusement value, right? To make me laugh...'

He didn't pretend the same incomprehension that she had earlier. '*Did* it amuse you? It didn't look like it. I thought you might be flattered at the idea that I chose you, out of all the beautiful women who have made themselves available to me—and they *do* make themselves available, Grace—to be my first and only lover. Instead you looked as if the frog you had just kissed had turned out to be fire-breathing dragon instead of the nice safe prince you had expected——'

It was exactly how she had felt. The waiter slid in and out and Grace looked helplessly at the plate of artfully arranged, unidentifiable food in front of her. But 'flattered' didn't begin to describe the turmoil of her feelings.

She felt a piercing thrust of possessiveness at the thought of being a 'one and only' in Scott's life, although the notion that any woman would ever be allowed to possess Scott Gregory was absurd.

'Is that why you said it? Did you think it was a fantasy of mine to... to——?' She stopped, suddenly aware how much she was revealing.

'Be the seducer rather than the seduced?'

Grace poked experimentally at her food with her fork, trying to ignore the provocative images his smoky murmur was generating in her overheated brain.

Brains? *Lamb's* brains?

Her unsullied stomach lurched as she identified her meal.

'I suppose it's a line that works with some women,' she said hurriedly, to take her mind off the concoction in front of her. 'But everyone knows that you... that you...'

He was eating his steak with fine appetite, regarding her with a politeness that didn't quite disguise his wretched enjoyment of her floundering attempt to obtain an answer without actually asking the pivotal question.

'You've been out with lots of women!' she finally managed to accuse him when it was obvious he wasn't going to help.

'Yes, I have,' he admitted with cheerful frankness.

'Well, then!' She glared at him. 'Don't tell me you didn't go to bed with some of them.' Her tone was re-inforced with patent disbelief.

'All right, I won't,' he said calmly.

'What does *that* mean?' she harried him.

'That you're obviously determined to believe what you want to believe.'

She opened her mouth and closed it again. She poked again at her food, shifting it on the plate.

'Grace, if you have something to ask me—ask,' he said gently, inexorably.

'Are you homosexual?'

If he was shocked by her bluntness he didn't show it. He merely grinned hugely. 'No.'

He waited, but she had reached a sticking point.

'Was I really *that* good, Grace?' he murmured blandly.

'Yes!' she hissed, goaded to the limit of her patience.

The lightness fell from him like a cloak, leaving him rawly exposed. A flush darkened his olive skin. His hand tightened on hers in a small act of possession.

'I'm flattered,' he growled huskily, and she had no doubt that he was. She felt an electrifying awareness. It was like being plugged directly into his central nervous system, experiencing his physical stimulation as if it were her own, bypassing other forms of communication. His eyes, hot and bold, were feverishly self-absorbed. Last night, as he had joined himself to her, he had looked just so...

For a moment Grace had a mental image of their entwined bodies, so powerful that she felt reality slip away. She closed her eyes in a shock of longing. The vivid memory of the rough crush of his mouth made her tremble and it was no surprise to open her eyes again and find that reality had superseded imagination. He kissed her lingeringly, with slow pleasure, his exultant desire singing on her tongue before he withdrew and visibly shook himself, grinning at her with an odd crookedness that made her heart melt.

'Sorry, I guess I got carried away there for a moment. You have no idea how it makes me feel to be accused of being such an incredible lover that I must be some kind of latter-day Don Juan. It almost makes up for the rest...'

'Oh, I think I can guess,' Grace said shakily, wondering what he meant by 'the rest', but afraid to ask. She became acutely aware of the surrounding murmurs and pulled her hand away from him, instantly missing the reassurance of its warmth.

'If this is your idea of not embarrassing me then I think you need a dictionary,' she said, making a valiant attempt to cool down.

'Consider it a salute to your femininity,' he replied, the husky note of desire still lingering in his voice as he turned and swept the room with a long icy stare that sent several avid faces diving for cover. Once again Grace felt herself distinguished by his powerful protection. Her warm sense of security lasted only a moment.

'Just think of the implications, though, if by any chance I'm *not* spinning you a line,' he pointed out softly. 'It would mean *you're* the one in control of our love-making. The woman who seduced my innocence with the irresistible warmth of her sensuous passion, who taught me everything that I know about the taking and giving of pleasure. The only woman in the world with whom I have shared the ultimate act of love...'

'*The ultimate act of love...*'

He made it sound utterly wicked and yet so infinitely desirable and right that Grace felt a slithery stirring of excitement. He made her *want* to be that sexy, sophisticated, worldly-wise and oh, so special woman. The one whose very uniqueness would bind him to her for all time, as his unforgettable *first...*

'Why aren't you eating?'

Grace came down to earth with a bump at the prosaic change of subject and followed his concerned gaze to her plate.

She shuddered her distaste. 'I didn't realise it was brains when I ordered. If it's true that you are what you eat then I think I'll settle for what intelligence I already have.'

'Would you like some of my steak?' He cut off a succulent slice and held it temptingly to her lips.

'Actually, I'm not very hungry,' Grace said hurriedly, ignoring the titbit. A kiss was a casual occurrence these days, but sharing bites of food from the same plate was still an act of public intimacy.

'At least eat your salad and bread roll. You can't go back to work on an empty stomach. I'll make sure that you have something nourishing for dinner tonight.'

'Dinner?' Excitement coiled in her empty stomach.

'Did you plan on our not seeing each other tonight, Grace?' he asked mildly.

She knew his calm was deceptive. A secret tingle of delight shot along her nerves. 'I—I have a class.'

'I know, the early one.' He knew her schedule as well as she did. 'You'll rush home and rush out again and be too tired to make anything but a stop-gap snack by the time you get home. You're not very skilled in the kitchen, are you, Grace?'

'I'm improving,' she said ruefully. 'My mother always thought that good grooming was more important than good domestic skills, and Jon and I always had a cook and housekeeper.'

She referred to her late husband with a casualness that was vastly reassuring to the man across the table.

'I'm good at hors-d'oeuvres, though, and I'm an excellent hostess,' she added defensively.

'The two absolute essentials of life,' he mocked gently, letting her know that the gaps in her domestic education didn't bother him a bit. 'Knock on my door when you get back and I'll have something hot and delicious waiting for you, something that I guarantee will stimulate your jaded appetite...'

Grace blushed delicately, and he murmured chidingly, 'No, not *that*, Grace. I'm talking about the *first* course. It needs to be something that will build up your strength and stamina... because I want you to be at the peak of your mental and physical condition for the start of your first-term exams next week.'

'Oh.' She scowled at him. After he had wound her up with his teasing innuendo she was disappointed that it had turned out to be a paternalistic lecture. She didn't want to be reminded of the looming tests.

She needn't have worried about his paternalism; his next words were decidedly unfatherly. 'Mmmm... Good good, stimulating intellectual discussion and plenty of healthy exercise is what you need. Fortunately you have someone at hand who can provide all three in one free package!'

'Free?' To flirt with him last night had been reckless, the response dangerously uncertain. To do so today was richly entertaining, the outcome blissfully sure...

He shrugged lazily, sharing her artless enjoyment of the moment. 'More or less. The cost would be negligible to a hard-nosed tycoon such as yourself...'

'I've had too good a teacher to accept such an improperly vague offer without doing thorough background research first,' she rebuffed him with a sly paraphrase of some of his own teaching.

His mouth twitched. 'Improper? Definitely. Vague? I thought my intentions were delightfully explicit. But by all means do your research. You have my permission to put me through the most *rigorous* clinical trials that your imagination can devise. I place myself utterly in your *experienced* hands...'

Fortunately the waiter saved Grace from having to think of anything to top his outrageous blandness. After fussing over her uneaten meal the waiter accepted, po-faced, Scott's assurance that it was the company rather than the food that she had found impossible to stomach. The lavish tip he accepted with equal aplomb. It was obviously restaurant policy to cultivate the eccentricities of its more influential and wealthy customers.

Outside, it was still gloomy, wet and cold but Grace felt the bright promise of the day. Scott was arrogantly trying to hustle her on her way so that she wouldn't get wet, the slight abstraction of his farewell indicating that his mind was already reaching ahead to his next ap-

pointment. Grace decided that it would be a mistake to
allow him to slot her into his life as if she were just
another responsibility to be crammed into his busy
schedule when it suited him. She had to assert herself
right from the start. She had worn her highest heels today
and to her secret delight was almost as tall as Scott. As
she turned to remonstrate she discovered that her mouth
was almost on a level with his, so it was entirely natural
that she should impulsively decide to take advantage of
the fact!

Right there on the rain-swept footpath she kissed him,
drawing wolf-whistles from the bored construction
workers huddled under cover across the street. When
Scott recovered from his surprise sufficiently to put his
arms around her Grace jauntily stepped out of the em-
brace and summoned a suitably blasé smile as she set
confidently off in the direction of her office.

'Consider it a salute to your masculinity,' she threw
over her shoulder, and didn't look back when she heard
him burst out laughing. She was rediscovering a joyous
spontaneity in herself. She had liked making Scott laugh
almost as much as she had enjoyed kissing him! Cold?
Restrained? Detached? The more she got to know him,
the more the gossips were disproved. What else had
rumour and gossip exaggerated? His sexual expertise?

Although the question nagged faintly at the back of
her mind, Grace pushed it away over the next two days,
enjoying too much the novelty of her passionate self-
indulgence. She was careful, however, to ensure that she
never overstepped the private line she had drawn in her
mind. Although they were lovers, they didn't live together
and Grace never assumed that Scott would always be
available to her... although he seemed to have no such
qualms. If she let him she had the feeling he would make
love to her all night and all day too. His passionate intensity, instead of diminishing with the frequency of their
lovemaking, seemed to grow even more voracious, as if

his appetite grew by what it fed on. However, the distinction was important for Grace's peace of mind. It meant that they weren't really *involved*. Except for the normal acts of courtesy, neither owed any responsibility to the other. That was the definition of a 'fling', and a fling was what she was having!

Her new image of herself as a sophisticated free spirit enabled her to deal coolly with Mabel's anxious maternalism and Neville's frosty disapproval at the office. She just ignored their well meant interference. Soon they, too, would realise that she was fully capable of coping with everything that life could throw at her. A mature, sophisticated businesswoman took such brief liaisons in her stride. The kind of devastating grief that she had felt after Jon died was not something she was anxious to feel again soon—if ever.

Thinking positively enabled her to weather the rather unpleasant shock of seeing herself identified a few days later, under a newspaper photograph of her with Scott at the Chamber of Commerce function, first as 'attractive companion of the elusive Mr Gregory' and further on as 'widow of electronics whizz Jonathan Blair' rather than as a person in her own right.

Shades of Lady Marlin! Grace thought wryly when Neville pointedly left the folded newspaper on her desk. But Lady Marlin, she told herself with a sneaking smugness, was definitely passé, while Grace was only just getting into her stride! To prove her indifference she cut out the item and sent it back to Neville with a wicked memo suggesting he might perhaps like to put it in the next in-house bulletin.

Mabel, typing out the memo, had commented sourly that perhaps she should enter it into the file that Mr Gregory himself had so kindly supplied them with.

That evening Scott took her to dinner at a very trendy wine-bar on the waterfront. It was crammed with trendy yuppies, the kind of noisy see-and-be-seen crowd that

Scott normally had nothing but contempt for, and Grace was surprised at his choice, particularly as he seemed strangely ill at ease as they had their pre-dinner drinks.

'We didn't have to come out tonight, Scott,' Grace said, watching as he downed two drinks with uncharacteristic speed and ordered a third. 'You don't have to entertain me if you've got other things on your mind— if there's something else you'd rather be doing.'

She tried to sound casual but in fact she had been sorely disappointed when he had suggested dining out, wondering for a brief, panicky moment if he was bored with her already. But then her confidence had reasserted itself. Last night they had eaten in front of a roaring fire in the living-room of his apartment and then he had made love to her on the hearthrug with his usual relentless energy. The heat that they had generated together had rivalled the fire for its melting fierceness. He had certainly not given any indication *then* of being bored!

He wasn't even aware of her, Grace realised broodingly. He was staring over her head at someone else, his being totally focused elsewhere. A friend? An enemy? *Another woman*? Her insecurity got the better of her. Gingerly, although she had the impression that she could have made a major production of it and Scott wouldn't have noticed, she turned and casually swept the room with wary blue eyes. No one stood out. No man glaring daggers at his corporate nemesis. No woman radiating any special glow.

Her overactive imagination again? She turned back to Scott. No. She shivered. The expression on his face reminded her of his look that day in her office, when they had shaken hands. There was a cold cruelty in the harsh set of his mouth, an oppressive contempt in the black eyes that verged on revulsion. Then he tore his gaze away from whatever—whoever—had riveted it and looked again into Grace's uneasy face. The change was extraordinary—like a quiet rejoicing. He didn't smile but she felt the gentle warmth of his regard like a physical caress flowing across her body.

'Scott——'

'I'm sorry——'

She didn't know what he was apologising for, but from the expression in his eyes she was going to find out. He was going to tell her something she didn't think she wanted to know. Instead he surprised her by saying abruptly, 'Shall we go?'

'Go!'

'Yes, *go.*' He pushed his drink away and stood, moving around to pull out her chair. 'You're right, I don't really want to be here. I don't want this after all...'

This? If she asked he might answer. Grace swallowed her treacherous curiosity and rose to follow him from the room, having to walk rapidly to keep up.

As they drew level with one of the tables near the door a husky feminine laugh drifted across their path and Scott's measured stride faltered.

'Scott, darling, what a surprise to see you here. Our paths never seem to cross these days. One might almost think that you were actively avoiding me!'

Another *older* woman! was Grace's first, fiercely jealous thought. She thwarted Scott's attempt to partly shield her with his body and moved up beside him to study the owner of the sultry drawl. She was beautiful, of course, her hair a clever shade of ash-blonde that flaunted rather than concealed the grey, her make-up so picture-perfect and grooming so flawless that Grace admired her devotion to her work, because it would be work to maintain that aura of immortal beauty and bold sensuality at...forty? Fifty?

'We obviously don't move in the same circles, Monique,' Scott was responding, his own voice totally devoid of any emotion. 'Perhaps because my tastes are little more *mature* than yours...'

This was accompanied by a cynical glance at the woman's companion, a handsome young man who blushed faintly as Grace looked at him. A very young man, Grace realised, having been at first misled by his elegant suit. He had only a bare suggestion of peach fuzz on his upper lip. Sixteen if he was a day and *not*, Grace guessed from Scott's remark, Monique's son or nephew...

'Mmm, yes, your speciality is grieving widows, I understand. Is this one of them?' Mocking green eyes flicked dismissively over Grace, a faint sneer distorting the ultra-smooth face as she watched Scott's hand come up to draw her imperceptibly closer to his side.

'No need to cringe, darling, I'm not going to soil your wounded little dove with tales from your murky past.' Her malice immediately made a lie of the taunting statement as it turned on Grace. 'But do be warned, my dear, that poor Scott isn't quite the shining example of manhood he seems. *I* blame that boarding-school of his—a hotbed of frustrated adolescent urges. And losing his mother, of course, at *such* a vulnerable age... Scott adored his mummy, didn't you, darling? He was—well—almost *unnaturally* attached to her. Even his father gave up trying to detach him from the apron strings...'

The woman moved from the merely crude to the utterly vile without pausing for an alcoholic breath. 'So you see, my dear, you're only part of a passing parade because what Scott is *really* after is a nice, safe, maternal womb to crawl back into, so the poor boy won't have to cope with the demands a *real* woman might make...'

Scott seemed untouched by the venom that sprayed from the beautiful bared fangs. The hand on Grace's elbow was relaxed, his tension of a few minutes before non-existent. In a strange way Grace felt his confidence permeate her mind and felt pity eclipsing her shock. To

be driven to such invective in public the woman must
be deeply unhappy.

'*Real* woman, Monique?' Scott mocked gently, then
turned aside her crudeness with a cool courtesy. 'As it
happens, I *am* looking for a mother—but for my
children, not for me.'

The beautiful mask tightened, revealing the prominent
bones of the skull beneath the skin, the lushly reddened
lips no longer looking full and sensual but standing out
like a livid scar of discontent, the eyes ugly with hatred.

Scott steered Grace back into motion as he said quietly,
with an air of cold finality, 'Good luck with the rest of
your life, Monique. I hope you find whatever it is that
you've been looking for so desperately all these years.
Son...'

He nodded to the boy, who was looking vividly embarrassed. The pointed farewell bypassed his reddened
ears but the woman seemed unwilling to let the conversation end.

'As if you care!' She directed her final comment to
Scott's indifferent back. 'Don't think I don't know you'd
like to see me writhe in hell. But you're no saint either,
so I guess we'll meet again after all!' Although her voice
was low and harsh, the accompanying laughter was hysterically shrill. A woman who lived very near the edge.

When they stepped out into the crisp evening air, Scott
took a long, deep breath, as if cleansing his lungs.

'You wanted me to meet her, didn't you?' Grace said
bluntly. 'That's why we came here tonight.'

'Yes. But when I saw her I realised I didn't want you
contaminated with her vileness. I haven't seen her for
two years but she hasn't changed a bit.' Without looking
at her Scott began to walk along the wide pavement,
past the food stands doing a brisk trade, to lean against
the iron railing overlooking the ferries moored at the
dockside. Several charters were taking boatloads of

merry-makers out into the harbour, but Scott and Grace ignored the shouts and waves.

'Why?' She joined him at the railing.

He took another deep breath and turned to face her, his hip still resting on the iron.

'I wanted you to see what she was like. So you'd understand.'

'Understand what?'

'Did you believe the things that she said about me?'

Grace didn't have to think; she shook her head. 'Why does she hate you? She was eaten up with it.'

'It's herself she hates,' he said simply, touching her puzzled mouth with a gesture that bespoke his gratitude for her trust. 'I just make a convenient focus. You might call me the one who got away.' His wry humour disconcerted her for a moment.

'You . . . you were lovers?' Ridiculous to feel as if it was a betrayal, but somehow the thought of him with that vile woman tainted *their* relationship.

'I wasn't capable at the time of being anyone's lover.'

Grace struggled to understand. 'She . . . You . . . you were impotent?' If he had had a sexual dysfunction then perhaps he had been telling her the truth about his virginity after all! Grace felt heat prickle across her forehead.

He smiled grimly. 'The word isn't applicable. I was a child.'

'A *child*?' Grace's exclamation was a gasp of horror. 'You mean, that woman——?'

'*That woman* is my father's widow. Monique Redman is my stepmother!'

CHAPTER NINE

'QUITE simply, she made my life a misery.'

Grace watched as Scott poured himself another brandy. It was on the tip of her tongue to tell him that he had already had more than enough, but she sensed that to continue his tale he needed to loosen the inhibitions that had leashed his inner rage for years. His need to tell her about the forces that had shaped his personality was even more profound than her need to know. And to listen without flinching was her responsibility. As his first lover she owed him that.

She knew now that the unthinkable was indeed the truth. As they had driven back to his apartment, under the concealing cloak of darkness and concentrating fiercely on the road ahead, he had told her how his mother's death had propelled him into a world with which he was ill equipped to deal. A warm and openly loving relationship with his mother had not prepared him for the cold discipline and social correctness that ruled his stranger-father's household, its emphasis on material wealth as the only measure of a person's worth and the deep adult resentments his presence provoked.

Newly married himself, to a woman a generation younger than himself, Lincoln Redman had gloated over his victory in gaining his son and yet had been selfishly impatient of any inconvenient demands on his attention. If Scott had spoken of his mother he had been punished, his grief dismissed as 'unmanly' and his childish views ridiculed.

Taking her cue from her husband, Monique Redman had treated the grief-stricken boy even more confusingly, frightening him with the unpredictability of her moods, either ignoring him totally or fawning embarrassingly over him. When his body had begun to show the first signs of manhood she had teased him mercilessly about it in front of her glamorous friends, pointing out the changes, touching him and making jokes and remarks that, at twelve, he didn't fully understand and yet which he sensed were deeply wrong within the context of their enforced relationship. She had intensified his embarrassment by drifting about the house in the semi-nude when his father wasn't there, invading Scott's room at unexpected times so that he had never felt secure of his privacy. After he had locked his door a few times when he was changing she had had the lock removed, telling her husband it was because Scott had taken to locking himself in his room and 'sulking like a girl' when he didn't get his own way. Lincoln Redman, always alert to any suggestion of improper behaviour in his son, had reacted in typical bullying fashion, lecturing Scott about what was expected of a 'real man' and brooking no excuses or explanations.

As the months passed Monique had realised that her husband's adoption of his son—the son who would now take legal precedence over any future male child that *she* might bear—didn't mean that he was willing to take on any day-to-day parental responsibility. The burden had fallen entirely on her resentful shoulders. Lincoln had travelled extensively on business and instead of taking Monique with him, as he had in the past, she had been forced to stay and 'look after' a boy she had increasingly resented. Her boredom and frustration had been expressed in ever more malicious taunting, until Scott had felt trapped in a morass of guilty confusion, afraid of the intensity of his dislike of his father's wife, and increasingly uncomfortable with his rapidly growing body.

'As far as Monique was concerned I was a convenient whipping-boy.' Scott handed Grace a brandy she hadn't asked for and she put it quietly aside as he sat back down beside her, staring into his glass, his face grim, remote.

'With my—with Lincoln away so much she could virtually do what she liked, knowing that even if I dared complain to him he would take her side over mine. She was clever. She'd make little disparaging remarks about my mother until I lost my temper and defended her. Of course, that made me a liar in my—*his* eyes because my mother was a stupid slut who chose life in the gutter to the advantages of a decent heritage for me. He *expected* me to rebel, even *wanted* me to, I think, because then he could punish me and therein by proxy punish the one who bore me. As it happened, Monique needn't have worried; I couldn't even explain my anxieties to myself, let alone anyone else. I just knew that I hated her and her rich, idle friends. They made me feel helpless, stupid and somehow *unclean*...'

'Wasn't there anyone you could have talked to?' Grace felt a deep compassion for his childhood anguish. She, too, had been used to satisfy a parent's desire to take revenge on the past. But although there had been an emotional closeness lacking in her relationship with her mother, she had never lacked for physical security. She had never been abused. And she had found the love that her young heart had craved with Jon...

He shrugged and the constriction around her heart tightened another notch. 'Oh, Scott...'

The tenderness in her soft exclamation seemed to rouse him from his grim introspection. His gaze snapped up to hers, male pride flaring at the expression on her face 'I'm not telling you this to gain your pity. It's in the past——'

'Is it?' Couldn't he see that his childhood insecurity haunted him still, through his vendetta against his father's company?

The black eyes gleamed with a ferocious satisfaction. 'I think *we're* proof of that...' His satisfaction inten-

sified as he watched Grace grow warm and flustered at
the hunger in his gaze.

'I don't want your pity, Grace. I just want you to know
why . . .' He motioned with his brandy glass, a sweeping
gesture that ended in another swallow. The muscles
clenched in his jaw as he drove himself on. 'When I
turned fifteen Monique decided that it was time I was
taught the facts of life . . . on a practical basis. She was
so self-absorbed and so used to manipulating her
husband with sex that it never occurred to her that a
young boy wouldn't be easy meat——'

Grace felt a hot tide of bile rise in her throat. 'Scott,
don't——'

She put out a hand to stop him torturing himself with
needless details but the bitter words spilled on. 'She timed
it very neatly . . . one day when I was changing out of my
school uniform. Unfortunately life isn't always so oblig-
ingly neat. My—Lincoln had cut short a business trip
and walked in to find me naked, clutching his semi-clad
wife as if I was trying to mount her rather than fight
her off——'

She thought the revulsion on his face was aimed at
his tormentor rather than himself until he said harshly,
'And the fact that I was erect utterly condemned me,
especially when Monique sobbed and showed him the
bruises on her arms where I had tried to hold her off. . .'

'Scott——'

'Yes, I was aroused!' he spat, his head half turned
away. Scott, who always faced a challenge directly, wasn't
equal to this one. 'I loathed her and what she was doing
but when she put her hand on me I responded . . .' He
shuddered with a remembered self-loathing that Grace
refused to permit.

'You mean your *body* responded. Scott, you were only
a boy, for goodness' sake,' she said gently. 'You had no
control over events, or over your own body for that
matter. Boys are notorious for the spontaneity of their

physical responses when they hit puberty. It was your hormones that responded to stimulation. Of *course* you got aroused...she touched you in a new and strange way deliberately for that effect. It's what's *supposed* to happen with men and women. But you were a boy, and you didn't have the mental control that men develop through experience, whereas she knew *exactly* what she was doing. For goodness' sake, surely you're not blaming yourself for that vile woman's perversion?' she exploded when he remained silent. '*She's* the one who was abnormal, Scott. It is quite, quite *normal* for boys to get wildly excited about sex before they really know what it's all about...'

There was something absurd about delivering a speech on adolescent male urges to a virile, fully grown adult man, and they both seemed to realise it at the same moment. Scott looked at her with a wry expression while Grace halted, thoroughly flustered and still fiercely angry on his behalf.

'I'm sorry, I didn't mean to lecture——'

'Who better?' he murmured over the top of his brandy glass. 'Of course you're right, I know that. But I didn't at the time. I felt as guilty of attempted rape as Monique accused me of being and got a thorough thrashing from my father for my sins. So thorough, in fact, that he cracked a couple of ribs.' He mentioned it casually, as if it hadn't mattered, and perhaps, in the utter turmoil of the time, it hadn't. 'He didn't even ask my side of it. He didn't want to know, especially when Monique tearfully took the opportunity to inform him she was pregnant.' He caught the hand that Grace raised to her shocked mouth and took it to his own.

'So then I was shunted off to a very distant boarding-school,' he said, his breath warm against the fleshy mound at the base of her thumb. 'An extremely Spartan last-resort school for the disgraced sons of the rich and famous. I stayed there even in holiday time. Needless to say, given the calibre of the students, bullying and anti-social behaviour was the norm. My guilt and revulsion about sex in general was reinforced by the crude boastings in the dorm and of course I was taunted and bullied for being ''different'', for not wanting to join even the most harmless sexual experimentation or discussion.' He drew her hand down to his hard thigh, squeezing her hand reassuringly as he watched the compassion soften her blue eyes while her vivid anger on his behalf still glowed in her cheeks. 'That school also gave me a lifetime distrust of the self-righteous probings of so-called ''experts''...psychologists and psychiatrists. Privacy is never more important than when you can't have it. Emotional and intellectual privacy is just as important as the physical kind. However, harsh as it was, being at school was better than being at home, so I stuck it out until I was old enough to go out on my own.'

'So you never...never told your father the truth?'

'After I left school we never saw each other again, except to spit and snarl at each other when our paths happened to cross in public. Monique miscarried and they never had any other children. No, I never told him the truth. As far as I was concerned, they deserved each other.' He drained his glass and bent to set it down by his feet.

'He didn't deserve a son like you,' Grace said quietly, her eyes tracing his hawkish profile.

'I wish I'd had your support then.' He put his other hand on hers, trapping it even more securely against his thigh. 'Of course, if I'd had you as a friend of my youth I wouldn't have stayed a virgin all these years...'

She still wasn't ready to joke about it. 'But your reputation...all those women...?'

'You of all people should know how misleading a reputation can be, Grace,' he said drily. 'And I suppose I encouraged the speculation by dating plenty of women. I guess it only took one of them to try to boost her self-

importance with her friends by giving them to believe
we were lovers for the rest to follow suit...not to mention
those disgruntled ladies who thought they could snare
some of my fortune by implying I had besmirched their
honour. You know, once I even had to fight a paternity
suit!' His smile was the slightly cruel one that she ab-
horred. 'Fortunately I won the case without having to
produce certified proof of my chastity.' He gave her a
hooded look. 'That extremity I've only been driven to
once in my life...'

He was referring to that provocative letter from his
doctor. Grace frowned in reproof of his flippancy.

'But...weren't you ever...tempted?' she enquired
delicately.

He wasn't embarrassed by the question. He turned his
body towards her, tucking her hand more comfortably
between his, seeming to relish the piquancy of the conversation now that the ugly part was behind him.

'When I was younger I was too busy proving to myself
that I didn't need my father's name or money to succeed.
I intended to show him who was the better man. Then,
too, I was very wary of the kind of woman who moves
in moneyed circles. I knew too well the hypocrisy and
corruption that easy wealth and a sophisticated lifestyle
can generate. Most of the women I date these days
remind me too much of Monique: selfish and super-
ficial, restless and congenitally unsatisfied, sexually
active and emotionally frigid, usually slaves to their own
avaricious desires. The sort of women who are all show,
entertaining to date, but if you let them close enough to
find a weakness they'll strip you like hungry piranha...'

Grace was slightly stunned by this sweeping condemnation. He smiled crookedly at her shock. 'You think I
exaggerate, but *en masse* that's what they're like. I date
them in sheer self-defence. And unfortunately the reputation it's gained me as a womanising heartbreaker tends
to frighten off all the nice, genuine, warm-hearted girls

who might really have seduced me out of my comfortable, asexual indifference. It's a vicious circle.'

'How awful for you,' Grace said tartly. Didn't he consider her a 'nice girl', then? 'And of course you've *hated* every moment of it!'

He was amused by the hint of hostility. 'Not *hated*— I'm not that perverse, Grace. Despite my uninterest in sex, I was fully capable of enjoying feminine company for its own sake. But I never felt so strongly attracted to any one of them that I was willing to allow myself to be vulnerable. In fact my virginity didn't really worry me at all until fairly recently. Perhaps something was freed in me when my father died, or perhaps it's because the closer I got to RedWing Industries the more I wondered what I would do *after* I had achieved everything that I had worked for for so long. I began to wonder whether the sexual part of my nature had been subliminated for so long that it would never find spontaneous expression. The first time began to loom as a rather daunting barrier. I decided that I had to make a concerted effort to breach it by the time I was thirty or I might never form a successful relationship with a woman...'

'So you started looking for someone to experiment on,' said Grace, his clinical assessment like a slap across her face.

Was he telling her that he was just using her to warm himself up for another woman? Her fingers curled in his grasp, unconsciously digging into his palm.

'No.'

She glared at him angrily. 'But you just said——'

'I'm giving you the background to my state of mind, Grace. As it happened, I didn't have to go looking at all. Something happened that made me realise I was wrong.'

'Oh? What?'

'A woman...'

Grace's eyes went from angry blue to sea-green wariness. He looked too smug for her to be comfortable.

'I didn't have to go out and find her because she found *me*. I walked into a lift and found a woman who was an erotic fantasy come to life. Sweetness and sin all tangled up in one electrifying fur-wrapped package. It was as if I'd stuck my finger into a light socket...excruciatingly painful but fantastically thrilling. I had dreams about her for weeks afterwards...achingly erotic, brutally satisfying dreams. I woke every morning on a physical high. I went around in a state of constant semi-arousal. Any doubts about my sexuality vanished like smoke in the wind. My body was in control and I revelled in it. You might say that my arrested adolescence was back on track—at full throttle...'

The lazy complacency faded with each succeeding sentence, becoming charged with a tension he made no effort to conceal. Grace began to tremble. There was no mistaking what he was telling her...the smouldering dark eyes as they drifted from her flushed face to the rounded thrust of her breasts under the soft bodice of her elegant sea-green dress made his meaning very explicit.

'I dreamt that I hadn't calmly buttoned that coat back up, Grace,' he said huskily. 'In my dreams we were alone and I did to you what I had wanted to do then—pushed you down on the carpet and pushed into you, swiftly and savagely like a conquering hero. In my dreams it was *me* you were wearing that fur coat for. It was me that the darling rosebuds were for. You were offering yourself to me freely. You were utterly mine and I rewarded you by being the best lover you had ever had...'

'A t-typical male fantasy,' Grace stuttered blindly, pulling away from him in a purely feminine flutter.

His smile was wolfish. 'And can you say that you had no correspondingly typical *female* fantasies about that night, Grace? No dreams about a safely anonymous,

virile stranger so stricken with lust by your beauty that
he ignores your protests and overpowers you with incredible pleasure, ravishing you to the brink of
madness . . .'

How could he know? Her embarrassment over the incident had been so acute that she had refused to acknowledge, even to herself, the forbidden thoughts that
had occasionally intruded on her subconscious.

He wouldn't let her evade him, letting her tensed hand
go to cup her chin and force her to look at him as he
guessed at her thoughts with painful accuracy.

'Don't. There's nothing wrong with having fantasies.
They're a natural and healthy form of release for people
like us, people who are lonely or hurting or who simply
aren't free to express their needs in more physical ways . . .
Of course, I had no idea then of who I was fantasising
about. I sometimes wondered whether you were real at
all, or if my fevered imagination had conjured the whole
thing up.' He let her chin go, but held her gaze with the
power of his own.

'Then I found out that not only were you real—but
you were also the very recent widow of someone whom
I had respected. It didn't sit well to discover I was lusting
wildly after a woman I was to have business dealings
with . . . or that you were evidently a lot merrier than
rumour and research had suggested. I, who considered
myself totally disillusioned about women, found that I
still had some illusions left. I came down to earth with
an uncomfortable thump. My fantasy woman was
another Monique—greedy, amoral and untrustworthy.'
His mouth curved in a humourless smile. 'I decided that
someone was going to suffer for that betrayal and it
wasn't going to be me. I even convinced myself I was
avenging your dead husband's honour. An expensive
young wife who plays around . . . you were probably the
reason for his shaky situation . . . possibly even his heart
attack. When I walked into your office that first day I

fully intended to rape the company and ruin you...and enjoy every minute of it!'

Grace was appalled by the savagery in his tone. He knew his early opinion of her was mistaken and yet here he seemed to be almost relishing the contemptible memory. What had she unleashed by taking him into her body? What would he do with the power that she had given him—over herself and over other women? Was she, after all, just an instrument of his revenge? Her first impulse was to flee both him and this new, desperate uncertainty.

Her action was so unexpected that she got as far as the door before Scott reacted. As she grasped the knob two arms came past her shoulders, caging her against the door.

'It's too late to run, Grace. It was too late the day we met.' She felt his breath warm against the exposed nape of her neck and didn't dare turn. She had worn her hair up this evening, in order to achieve the elegant and sophisticated look that she thought her urbane lover deserved, but tonight the usual confidence trick wasn't working. She still felt gauche, unbearably susceptible to all the bitter nuances of his mood.

'Please. I want to go home,' she whispered to the cool blank surface of the door.

'I can't let you do that.' He moved his body closer, so that she felt him all the way down her spine. His hands moved, almost overlapping on the painted wood so that his arms crushed the soft sides of her breasts. 'I can't let you go thinking that I have everything I want from you. I don't. It's too late for me, too, Grace. I couldn't crush that initial automatic sexual response, no matter how much I tried. And I tried only until I realised that there was a spirited, passionate woman behind the stunning fantasy. A woman who, like me, was hiding her true nature behind a protective mask...who was warm and vulnerable and trying desperately not to be, not to need or to want...'

Grace could feel herself melting, folding back against his hard body as the wistful words wrapped themselves around her heart, constricting her chest and starving her of the oxygen her brain needed to assimilate this startling new development. He sounded almost as if...as if—— She slammed the shutters down on the forbidden thought.

'I should go,' she said, but weakly, courting the danger.

'How can you abandon me now, when I need you so much...?' With a quick, clever movement he spun her in his arms and then his mouth was covering hers. His hands moved over her back and the constriction in her chest eased as the zip parted along her back. His fingers pulled back the jersey fabric and stroked over her bare skin, dipping down to press into the dimples at the base of her spine, arching her slightly so that her shoulders fell back, allowing the slippery fabric of her dress to slide to the top of her breasts. The taste of him exploded inside her mouth, filling her senses with an intoxicating warmth and aroma that had nothing to do with the amount of brandy he had consumed. He made sounds— rough, greedy, indistinct sounds that vibrated through her tissues, his lips and teeth and tongue consuming her with his passion. Grace felt her doubts and fears slide away, as they always did when he took her in his arms, to be replaced by a hunger that fought with his for supremacy. She moaned when, after drinking his full from her parted mouth, Scott broke free, but he was only shifting his grip so that he could explore the creamy exposed slopes of her breasts, one arm curving rigidly to support her waist as he arched her further, planting his powerful legs on either side of hers to balance their combined weight as he teased her with his aching restraint. Even when she begged him in husky tones of sensual abandonment he only slowly dragged aside the pretty cream camisole that was all she wore beneath the loose-fitting bodice of her dress. He made her wait as he arranged the lace to frame her aching breasts to his artistic satisfaction, holding her arched helplessly across his arm, her head hanging down, weighted with dizzying images of what he was going to do next. He heightened her excitement, and his, by making her wait an excruciatingly long time before he finally touched her, a gentle, moist, sliding salute of his tongue against the rigid, rosy peaks. After each slow stroke he paused to ask her thickly if she wanted more, flexing his thighs languidly between hers, teasing her with the fullness of his manhood until her hands blindly ripped at the thin silk of his shirt and he generously gave her what she pleaded for—the soft, rhythmic suckling that drew the piercing sweetness from her swollen breasts and pooled it between her thighs. Finally, when she was shaking so much that he staggered with the violence of her pleasure, he drove her back against the wall and took her as she stood, careless of the clothes that bunched between them, oblivious to everything but the primitive, driving force that had conquered him far more devastatingly than he had conquered her.

Afterwards, Grace was slightly horrified at the frenzied haste of their coupling. She primly straightened her twisted dress and blushed when Scott gravely helped her untangle her underclothes and calmly zipped her back up.

'It's late,' she murmured awkwardly.

'Stay.'

His voice made it a request, but his eyes made it a command.

'I—I can't...'

'Am I so easy to walk away from, Grace?'

The faint trace of wistfulness contrasting with the determination in his eyes was almost her undoing. But she *had* to walk away. If she stayed, who knew what further weakness he might find to exploit?

'Of course not,' she told him the truth calmly. He would know a denial for a lie anyway. 'But I still have a lot of studying to do. My exams, remember?'

'I could help you study,' he offered with a diffidence that didn't quite mask the frustration.

'Thank you, but no,' she said gently but firmly, relieved to see that he was taking the rejection calmly. She had to remember that, for all his worldliness, in the realm of sexual relationships Scott was a novice. If she didn't handle the situation carefully she might cause further trauma to his masculine ego. Scott, more than most men, would need to remember his first lover with a pride and satisfaction untainted by any hint of failure if he was to fully escape the inhibiting consequences of his tormented adolescence and find lasting contentment with another woman. *Another woman...* Grace gritted her teeth. She had no right to feel jealous. No right at all. It wasn't healthy... She was doing this for his own good!

'I really do need some proper rest. I—I'll see you tomorrow...'

'See me?' His black eyes sliced through her fragile calm. 'Or have sex with me?'

After their physical closeness of a few minutes ago, Grace was shocked by the contempt in the crude phrase. 'Scott——'

'Well, isn't that what you meant? God forbid we should call it anything else...liking making love...'

Grace swallowed. 'Don't be like this, Scott——'

'Like what? A human being? I'm not a machine, Grace. I'm a man. I'm your lover. And I want more from you than this constant...withdrawal. And, dammit, you want more too! Only you're too damned afraid to ask...'

'Ask what?' Unconsciously she was backing away from him, but this time he let her, his eyes locking with hers.

'Why *you* ...'

'Why me?' she repeated faintly, guardedly, drawn to a halt by the sheer power of his will as he answered quietly,

'Because I'm in love with you, of course ...'

Of all the things she had braced to hear him say, this was so far down the list that she hadn't even considered it!

The words hit her like a blow, so nearly physical that she actually rocked on her feet. Her flushed face paled and then flushed again, her eyes a wide, bewildered blue. The rotation of the world seemed to speed up, weighting her limbs to an alarming degree.

'In love?' She formed the words thickly, clumsily, but Scott had no difficulty in understanding her.

'Yes—love. You know, that warm, wonderful feeling that—— '

'You can't be!' The world stopped dead. Gravity ceased to exist. Now Grace thought she might float off into endless, velvety-black space. But he was there to catch her, touching her softly where the pulse throbbed wildly in her throat.

'Why not?'

'Because ...' She was too breathless to convince him of his confusion. Her pulse bucked boldly under his monitoring thumb. 'Because it wasn't supposed to be like this ... we're just having an affair——'

'A *love*-affair.'

She ignored him, continuing doggedly, 'You—you wanted to find out about sex and I ... I—was missing——'

'A stud in your bed?'

She glared at him.

'So I was your idea of an uncomplicated roll in the hay?'

Her glare became a blush of guilt. No one in their right minds would call Scott Gregory uncomplicated, and he knew it. Knew that whatever her prevarications there had been more to it than that. Grace drew herself up authoritatively. 'It's quite natural, you know,' she told him firmly.

He folded his arms across his chest, content that she had stopped trying to escape and was instead trying to reason her way out of the trap she didn't even seem to realise had closed tightly around her some time ago.

'What is?'

She waved her arms helplessly. 'You thinking that you're in love with me. It's only because I...you...' There was no way to put this delicately, so she snapped tersely, 'Because I was your first woman.' The blunt statement gave her such a warm, possessive feeling that she blundered furiously into further trouble. 'I mean...everyone is very intense about their first lover...and with you it would be especially so. I mean, I was the one who freed you from your inhibitions... It's all new and exciting to you and naturally you feel, well, relieved and...and *grateful*——'

'Gratitude...' he mused grimly. 'Is that all *you* felt when you and Jon first made love...?'

She jerked. 'No, of course not!'

'Because you were in love,' he agreed gently. 'It makes a difference, doesn't it? Maybe not one you can readily explain but it's there just the same; the *rightness* of joining physically with that one particular person...'

Grace moistened her dry lips. 'You don't love me!' she protested huskily.

'Tell yourself that often enough and you might believe it,' he murmured sardonically.

'But I don't *want* you to love me!' she cried desperately. If she accepted the validity of his emotions then she might have to question the frightening shallowness of her own. Only a year ago she had been desperately wanting to give her husband a child. The love she had given Jon had been guiltless, sweet and selfless, a stable force in their marriage that had enabled them to weather the disappointment of their childlessness. It bore no resemblance whatsoever to the exhausting storms of rage and delight that confused her when Scott was taunting or arousing her, the selfish abandonment and reckless passion that led her to lose all sense of shame and propriety. That was why she knew that what she felt couldn't be love. Not any kind of love that she recognised, anyway, and she was surely more of an authority than Scott!

'Don't you?'

The simple question terrified her.

'I told you—it's far too soon...I never thought I—I thought that you——' She got a grip on herself, twisting her weakness into a desperate accusation. 'You said you weren't going to ask for my love!'

'I lied,' he stated with a devastating lack of remorse. 'I didn't want to scare you off. At that point I wanted you so badly that I would have said anything in order to have you. Well, I'm done with lying. I *want* you to feel threatened, if that's what it takes to get a genuine reaction out of you. I won't let you make me ashamed of my feelings. I twenty-nine, not nineteen. This isn't a boyish infatuation that I'm going to grow out of. If you want more time to think about it, fine, I'll back off for a while. But don't ask me to make it easy for you...'

CHAPTER TEN

'IT'S sexual blackmail!'

Grace's voice was shrill with frustration and there was a brief, telling pause at the other end of the telephone.

'It's hard for me too, honey... quite literally, in my case.'

Scott's amused tone infuriated her, particularly when she knew he probably meant it. Grace stared hard at her desk-top, trying to distract herself from the erotic image of Scott sitting at his desk on the other side of the city, aroused from wanting her.

In the last three weeks she had come to appreciate what a consummate master Scott was at 'not making it easy' for her. In love, as in everything else, he had proved to be ruthless.

It *should* have been easy. If she had been one of Monique's ilk, it would have been. A few ugly words to chisel at his pride, a show of cold indifference to his need, a cruel mockery of his naïveté... Scott had revealed enough of himself to give Grace plenty of ammunition to mortally wound him. But she couldn't use the weapons knowingly placed in her hands. She had been ensnared by a simple act of trust from a man who had built an empire on his mistrust of people—women especially. He knew that his expression of love would render her powerless to attack him.

Powerless but not totally helpless. It *was* just an infatuation on his part. Sooner or later he would realise it and then he would be relieved that she hadn't taken him seriously. The best way to handle the impossible situation, Grace decided, was to do nothing. Humour him. Enjoy the transient happiness he offered until the obsessive sexual attraction had run its natural course and they could both view it more objectively, as the aberration it most certainly was.

She might have known that Scott would be two steps ahead of her!

She gripped the telephone receiver hard, fighting for self-control. Oh, he still wooed her like a lover, pandering to her in public and pampering her in private, altogether taking up a disturbing amount of her time whether he was physically present or not.

But he *wasn't* a lover.

Scott had refused to make love to her again until she was prepared to commit more than just her body to their relationship!

He didn't want to just live for the moment. He was demanding a place in her future. What that 'place' should be he hadn't specified. He didn't need to. He knew what kind of woman she was. If she made the kind of mental commitment he was asking then, whatever form of relationship resulted, she would honour it with the same loyalty and integrity with which she had honoured marriage. She would be relinquishing her recently acquired independence, cutting her ties to a past love and putting her trust in an uncertain future. She would be admitting that she loved him completely and without reservation. She couldn't make herself achieve the final, giant leap of faith that that required...

'If you loved me as much as you *say* you do you wouldn't be able to do this!' Grace could hardly believe the trite cliché that spilled out of her mouth.

Judging from the choked sound at the other end of the line, Scott couldn't either.

'That desperate, huh, Grace?' His voice slid an octave lower, a husky thrust of desire. 'I know exactly how you feel. But we virgins believe in upholding our principles and respecting our bodies——'

'Principles!' Grace exploded. 'You don't have any principles. And you're not a virgin any more, either!'' she added cuttingly.

'Thanks to you, Grace.' She could imagine his dark eyes narrowing sexily with mocking amusement. 'I hope you're not suggesting that I should start sleeping around?'

'Of course not!' she bit out.

'I see. You want me to sleep only with *you*,' he clarified softly.

Yes! He was hers, dammit! Even as she thought it she realised the appalling selfishness of her jealousy. She had refused to love him as he deserved to be loved—but she didn't want anyone else to have him either. 'I——'

'Perhaps we could discuss it over dinner?'

Grace almost groaned out loud. Another cosy dinner at an intimate restaurant or his apartment, exchanging polite chit-chat and duelling expressions while their bodies ached to be engaged in a duel of a different kind! Another chaste kiss at her door, making her aware of the physical closeness that she was denying them both.

'Sorry, but I have to work late tonight. Perhaps another time.' She hung up crisply before he could tantalise her any further. He had a habit of doing that. Hinting that a little more coaxing on her part might change his mind. Challenging her to try to seduce him all over again. To her shame it was a challenge she had found almost impossible to resist. Before, where she had only wanted, now she *craved*... The shakes and sweats and night horrors of addiction were truly frightening, for they implied an emotional as well as a physical dependency.

If she hadn't had her work and her studies she would have been a mess. At least at the office she could feel comfortably in control of herself, and her exam results had removed any doubts about her competence. She wasn't near the top in any of her classes, but she wasn't

at the bottom, either. Next time she was determined to
do even better.

The early-winter darkness was drawing in as she drew
the last stack of papers towards her, glancing up to see
Mabel at the door.

'Haven't you left yet?' Grace looked at her watch.
'It's gone six o'clock. I thought I told you to go home
ages ago.'

'I had a few letters I wanted to finish.'

It might or might not have been the truth. More likely
it was her secretary's overdeveloped motherly instincts
at work.

'Oh, well, I'm just about finished myself,' Grace murmured, wondering if she dared sleep the night on her
office couch. If she went home she would inevitably see
Scott and her defences were definitely shaky right now.
She needed to think, to plan, to come to terms with the
chaotic nature of her feelings before she faced him again.

Mabel made her disapproval clear as she fetched her
coat and shrugged into it, lingering to add, 'I hope you're
not going to turn out to be as much of a workaholic as
Mr Blair was. I haven't seen you looking so pale since
you first came to work here. You should relax
more——'

Grace's reply lodged in her throat as a man walked
through from the outer office and gently moved the older
woman out of the way. 'Exactly what I've been telling
her, Mabel. Why don't you go home and let me look
after your ewe-lamb?'

'I'm afraid she doesn't take orders very well.' Mabel's
concerned face softened into wry amusement as she
turned to obey Scott's suggestion.

'Ah, but she doesn't pay my salary. She can't fire me
for insubordination. Have a nice evening, Mabel.'

'Goodnight.' The smile Mabel directed at him was
almost coy, thought Grace in disgust. A month ago
Mabel would have bristled with hostility if Scott had

suggested knowing Grace better than she did. But since then he had put himself out to charm. Even Neville's defensiveness had largely vanished, as Blair Components began to show a healthy optimism in its cash flow as a result of the organisational changes Scott had suggested.

'I told you I was busy——'

'I know what you told me. I only called in to tell you that I'm dining out tonight, so you don't have to hang around here trying to avoid me.'

She decided it would be futile to argue. The model haughtiness that deceived everyone else had never fooled Scott. She studied him sourly. He must have been home to change, because he wasn't wearing the same suit he had been wearing when she had seen him climb into his car in that morning. There was also something about him, a daunting new grimness in the dark, brooding expression. Her empty stomach lurched sickeningly, hot jealousy flooding her tight throat. Had he finally given up on her? Found another woman, warm and willing, to satisfy his deeper needs?

'No.'

'No what?' she asked hollowly, staring fixedly at his immaculate white shirt-front until he leaned down against the desk so that his face dropped into her field of vision.

'No, I'm not seeing another woman, Grace,' he told her with steely patience. 'But I *do* feel like some relaxed companionship tonight, so I'm going to attend a stag dinner at my club. *Now* will you go home?'

There was a small, stricken silence. 'I just have these few papers to look through,' Grace muttered, shuffling them.

'Take them with you. Here's my key.' There was a small, metallic click as he laid it on the polished surface of her desk. 'There's a casserole for you in the oven.'

'You don't have to do this. I can take care of myself,' said Grace, reluctantly picking up the key. It was still warm from his hand. His generosity made her feel small and petty, as no doubt he intended.

'I don't do it because I *have* to, Grace, I do it because it gives me a great deal of satisfaction.' He straightened abruptly, his patience curdling into acid. 'But of course I was forgetting that caring for you is taboo. I'm permitted to do everything except love you—*that* would be indecent. I get to bed you, entertain you, feed you, advise you, send you a few token flowers——'

He stopped, his mouth tightening. He cursed, half turning away, halting as he saw the huge vase of roses under the window.

'Two dozen roses a day for the past fortnight is hardly a mere token,' Grace said, pouncing on his slip. She had given them away to Mabel and the other office girls at first but, like Scott himself, the avalanche of flowers was relentless, their exquisite fragrance hauntingly pervasive, their velvety beauty subversive. The usual anonymous delivery had continued to vary but this new, extravagant tribute was always the same: sheafs of bluish-pink rosebuds, delicate, perfect, and alarmingly evocative.

'Rather hypocritical of you not to include a message, isn't it?' Grace probed softly, rising to join him, determined to settle this once and for all. 'Considering your opinion about anonymous gifts.' But of course they hadn't been anonymous, not really. Pink rosebuds were a message in themselves. A wicked reminder of all they shared. Stubbornly she had refused to acknowledge the message, and his fresh assault on her consciousness had never been mentioned.

His mouth twisted bitterly. 'Did you think they were from your secret admirer?'

She hesitated. 'And aren't they?'

He looked at her, taking in the tremulous mouth and the wide blue eyes that held a promise of paradise for the price of a small sin. He drew a harsh, rattling breath.

'I don't think my admiration of you is a secret any more,' he said bluntly.

Grace's eyes darkened to the colour of a sea-mist, a soaring sense of relief giving wing to her heart. 'I knew it! You never actually denied it, did you? Not in so many words. You just diverted my suspicions by pretending to be angry. But I think some part of me always hoped...always knew that they were from you...' Her shoulder brushed his as she stroked one of the long-stemmed roses wonderingly, suddenly unbearably shy under his brooding gaze. 'Why didn't you tell me?'

'Does it really matter, Grace?' he rasped. For an instant he looked as if he wanted to rip the rose from her fingers and trample it underfoot, and she was startled. Why was he so angry? He must have meant her to find out some time.

'Of course it does.' Instead of placating him, her eagerness seemed to trigger an even greater fury.

'Why? Do you feel safer with a rosy romantic fantasy to veil the raw physical reality? Is the love of a flesh-and-blood man not enough for you?'

Bewildered by his unexpected reaction, Grace tried to explain her confusion of feelings. 'I—it's just that the flowers were sort of a precious, private thing...a symbol of renewal, I suppose, a reminder that there was still beauty in the world if I cared to look for it. That was all I wanted it to be at first, but later I...well—I realised that they had started arriving just after we met in that lift. It seemed like far too much of a coincidence, especially when you were so attentive...'

Her eyes were opened to a whole new and liberating perspective on their breathtakingly sudden affair. 'You've been a part of my life for months, even though I didn't realise it. You've waited for me that long. And you didn't pressure me, not when you knew I wasn't ready for it, you just gave without expecting anything in return...and then I—I was such a bitch to you...'

She turned her back to the roses, lifting her hands to rest them pleadingly against his upper arms, feeling the iron-hard tension in his bunched muscles. 'I'm sorry, Scott... How I must have hurt you. If I had known...'

The glittering black eyes hooded, but not before she had seen the triumphant fire that briefly blazed in their depths.

'Does it make a difference to the here and now?' he demanded tightly.

She couldn't blame him for his wariness. 'You know it does.' She leaned her head briefly against his chest, feeling the shuddering tempo of his heart. 'I was so afraid of making a mistake, of rebounding into a relationship, any relationship, just to fill up the emptiness inside...of having to go through that grieving sense of loss *twice*... But you knew that. You put your own needs aside and then, when you manoeuvred our second meeting, you helped me to build my self-confidence by challenging me to fight for whatever it was I thought I wanted. You showed me how to let the past go, knowing that I could have ended up hating you for it...'

Deep colour had mounted his olive cheekbones as she spoke, his mouth thinning into a compressed curve, his slitted eyes avoiding hers. Did he think she would laugh at him for his incredibly romantic gesture? Her heart melted with tenderness.

'Oh, Scott——'

'Oh, *hell*——'

He kissed her.

It was rough, deep and devouring, full of repressed violence and lingering anger. When it was over he pushed her away and straightened his tie with hands that she was fiercely glad to see were trembling. So it was with shock she saw him glance at his watch and say thickly, 'I'm running late. I promised to be there by seven. Can we postpone this discussion until tomorrow?'

Grace couldn't believe that he would walk away when he was on the brink of total victory. He must be able to see that she needed to talk, to tell him what she felt, and to hear that he hadn't changed his mind. She stroked his wrist in a tiny, bold caress.

'Do you have to go?'

She felt his pulse leap against her fingers but he jerked away, saying tautly, 'I made a commitment...'

And when Scott gave his word, it stayed given. Grace felt the sweet knowledge sink deep into her uncertain soul. 'Will you come over afterwards? I'll wait up for you,' she said huskily.

'Better not. These things can go on all night,' he said with an icy reserve that she might have interpreted as crushing indifference if she hadn't been reading the subtle language of his body, the straining tightness of his jaw that had crippled his usual fluency, the stark hunger that stiffened his limbs and gave his stride an almost painful precision as he made for the door. 'Go home, Grace. We'll finish this tomorrow.'

He practically fled. Grace imagined she could hear his solitary, wolfish howl echoing along the corridors of the empty building.

She was smiling contentedly to herself as she put on her coat and picked up her handbag and drifted dreamily out to the empty reception area, her stack of unfinished work forgotten on her desk. Jon would approve, she felt. How could he not when Scott had held such a tender regard for the delicate balance of her loyalties?

'What's going on? Have you and Gregory had another fight?'

She hadn't realised that Neville was still in the building. Now she was working more independently she often went whole days without talking face-to-face with him.

'No, what makes you say that?'

'He just went past me like a bat out of hell.'

'He's late for an engagement.'

'And he's not taking you?' Neville bristled. He might not approve of her and Scott spending so much time together but he was firmly in favour of Grace's happiness.

'It's at his club—a night out with the boys.' Grace's voice was soft with an indulgent amusement that snapped her colleague to attention.

'My God, you're in love with him!' Neville looked momentarily appalled at the revelation.

'Would that be so awful?'

'I—I don't know!' To his eternal credit he didn't mention Jon. 'But... are you sure? You've only known him a couple of months and that seems to be about his attention span where women are concerned...'

A secret smile gave Grace's expression a bright piquancy. 'A bit longer that that, actually. He's the one, Neville—the person whose been sending me the flowers... Oh, not just the roses...' she added as he opened his mouth '... the others, too. Scott is my secret admirer!'

Neville paled. 'Did he tell you that?'

'Yes.' Grace laughed and danced a little twirl. 'Don't you see, Neville? I've already outlasted the others. It's not just a passing impulse for him. It's lasting, it's *real*...'

'Grace——'

'I don't know what he wants. I mean, I don't know if it means marriage but I don't care——'

'Grace——'

'He's even mentioned babies. When a man does that he's not just playing around——'

'*Grace*!' She stopped her joyous musing and stared at Neville's white face as he stated starkly, 'Scott is *not* your secret admirer.'

'Of course he is; he told me he——'

'He's *not*! Believe me, Grace, at this moment I wish he were, but he's *not*. And if he lied to you about that, what else has he been lying about?'

'You're wrong, Neville.' Grace felt battered. She hadn't realised how deep Neville's dislike of Scott went. So deep that he was prepared to destroy her chance of happiness...?

'I'm not wrong. And I can prove it.'

His quiet sincerity stunned her as did the thought that inevitably followed. 'You're not saying that...that *you*——?'

'No, no, of course not.' He shrugged off the suggestion with an impatience that shared the distaste she had felt for the idea.

'Then I don't understand.'

'Maybe we should go into your office——'

'There's no one around, Neville. Tell me here. *Tell me!*' Her voice rose to an almost hysterical shrillness. 'For goodness' sake, you're frightening me! How shocking can it be, unless you've discovered it's some homicidal lunatic——?'

Hours later Grace sat in the darkness of Scott's apartment, going over and over what Neville had told her, looking for the loophole that would explain everything, vindicate the man she loved from the squalor of a self-serving lie. There was none.

The initial numbness had passed a long time ago, superseded by a towering rage that had driven her to his apartment to belatedly turn off the oven that had burned his generous offering to a crisp. Generous? Yes, he could afford to be, when trading on another man's account!

No wonder he had been unable to look her in the eye. No wonder he had been so keen to get away. His conscience must have been burning like fire...if he even *had* a conscience!

And she had fallen in love with this unscrupulous liar! She had opened herself up to love only to find pain instead, but it was too late to protect herself by denying it.

A key in the lock wrenched her out of her trough of bleak despair.

She rose to her feet as Scott shut the door and switched on the light, blinking in owlish surprise at her. He frowned, thrusting his hands into his pockets and hunching his shoulders.

'I told you not to come here.' He was swaying slightly and that, plus his blurred syllables, told her that his dinner had probably been as much liquid as solid.

'But then, you tell me so many things, Scott,' she said with acid sweetness. 'How am I to know which of them to believe?'

He shook his dark head briefly, as if he couldn't quite believe what his glazed eyes were seeing. She was still wearing the steel-grey suit that she had been wearing earlier in the evening when he had reeled her in like the gullible fool she was. Her power-suit. What a laugh *that* was!

She knew a better way to clear his head. She took two steps forward and struck him, open-handed, across his lying face.

'What the——?' He staggered back, cupping his red-dened jaw. It took him less than a second to recover, planting his legs wider, tilting his torso towards her, his shoulders squared for battle, visibly struggling to focus his scattered thoughts and succeeding through sheer force of will. Even partly drunk he had more self-control than most men in full possession of their senses.

'What in the devil was that for, Grace?' he demanded sourly. 'What unwritten law of propriety had I broken this time? Having a few drinks too many? Do you blame me? I don't know if I'm on my head or on my heels half the time with you . . .'

'I know where I'd like to see you. Head-*over*-heels—in hell!' Grace yelled, aware she had totally lost control. She had promised herself that she wouldn't do this—get wildly emotional and let him see how much he had hurt her. Any minute now she would be bursting into weak tears and she had vowed she would never be weak again.

She tried to dash past him. It had been a bad idea to sit here, brooding away the dark hours of the night, attacking him when she was still so horribly vulnerable herself.

'Oh, no, you don't!' His hand was like a manacle on her wrist as he swung her around and brought her hard against his chest, his other arm slamming down like an iron bar across her slender back. 'You're not going anywhere until you've damned well explained yourself——'

'Explained *myself*?' She laughed bitterly into his handsome face. 'What is there to explain? That I've been a fool? Well, *you're* the fool if you think that I'd ever respect a man like you, let alone *love* him...' She spat out the word as if it was loathsome to her taste.

A brutal expression savaged his face. He'd had just enough to drink to smash his normal inhibitions. 'You mean a living man as opposed to a dead one? I thought we'd settled all that.'

She shuddered at the crude thrust. 'I mean an *honest* one, you liar!' she hissed. 'You filthy rotten *liar*!'

Scott felt the precipice of awareness open beneath his feet. He refused to jump. 'Why don't you put it into words of one syllable, Grace? I'm having difficulty following your ravings.'

'*Liar*!' She struggled fruitlessly against his superior strength, half sobbing her angry shame. 'You told me that *you* sent me the flowers. You let me believe... It wasn't you at all! You had nothing to do with it—except to steal another man's honour.'

'What makes you so sure?'

Oh, God, even now he was trying to wriggle out of it.

'Neville. He told me. You didn't send those flowers. My *husband* sent them!'

Fresh guilt rose up to smother her with its suffocating implications.

It was Jon who had been responsible for the gesture that had melted her frozen heart for another man. Neville, who had been sworn to reluctant silence, had even shown her a copy of the secret codicil to Jon's will. Her husband had established a special fund to provide for the delivery of flowers to Grace once a week for a year following his death. Secret, he had told Neville, because he had wanted her to enjoy them without sadness. Neville had continued to be loyal to his friend's memory, despite his misgivings. Grace had not.

'You *have* no husband,' Scott grated, shaking her with a violent movement of his own body. 'Dammit, Grace, that codicil was the product of an unhealthy obsession——'

'You're a great one to talk about unhealthy obsessions—with your twisted notions of getting revenge on your dead father and your...your sexual——!' Before she went too far the import of his words sank in and Grace went red, then white with shock.

'You knew!' she choked in horror. 'You *knew* about the will. Oh, my God...you *knew* you were taking credit for something Jon's love had given me——!' She put a hand over her mouth and he dragged it away.

'Love?' he snarled, his breath whiskey-hot against her face. 'Is *that* what you call it? What kind of love tries to cling on to a wife from beyond the grave? I can understand him being possessive of you when he was alive.' A harsh groan escaped him. 'Oh, *God*, can I understand it! But even in death he wasn't willing to let release you from your vows...he wasn't giving, he was trying to *take*——!'

'No!' Grace shook her head wordlessly, but he was in the grip of a wildness to match her own.

'*Think* about it! He made a generous provision for an ongoing memorial to himself and yet he left no provision for the living, for the woman he had supposedly loved so selflessly. It obviously didn't even occur to him that the gesture could have frightened or upset you. I bet he even *wanted* you to find out who sent them. Expected it. You could have, you know. All it took from me was a bit of pressure and leverage with the right people.

'And *yes*, I traded on that knowledge! Because I could see how much you wanted to weave me into your romantic fantasy. You wanted love in your life again—with *me*!—whereas what Jon wanted was for you to keep your grief fresh, to feel he was still watching over you, still a husband. If you had known those flowers were from him it would certainly have stopped you developing a healthy relationship with any other man——'

'Surely you're not calling what we have *healthy*?' Grace cried scornfully, hating him at that moment for pinpointing Jon's faults with such cruel accuracy. Why wasn't he showing any remorse for *his* selfish duplicity?

'Two emotional cripples like us could never hope to have a normal relationship!' she struck out wildly. 'We were *using* each other for a while, that's all, and it got out of hand——'

'Well, there's one sure way of finding out,' Scott grated, lifting her off her feet so that she had to clutch at his hard chest to stop herself sinking into his arms. Their eyes locked and Grace curled her hands into claws as he began to move.

'I'll fight you——'

He bared his teeth. 'Will you?'

In his bedroom he set her down, bending her arm forcefully, but not painfully, behind her back.

'You can't do this——!'

'Watch me.'

She couldn't help it. He was stripping off his clothes one-handed, the look in his black eyes so searingly familiar that she felt her anger shudder and fail.

'No——' she protested raggedly, trying to block out the impact of his magnificent nudity. To her dismay, he suddenly released her, stepping back, lying down on the smooth cover of the bed, naked and unashamed.

'Come on, Grace, use me.'

Grace was bereft in a freedom she suddenly discovered she didn't want. 'W-what?'

She and Jon had rarely argued, and never this tempestuously. They had buried their differences instead of airing them. Only with Scott had she learned to fully appreciate the bitter-sweet, heart-piercing pleasure of making up...

'Use me, Grace. If that's what we've been doing so far, I love it. I want to be used. Now.' He stretched, a long ripple of pure muscle as he invited her in a throaty purr that wrapped itself around her heart and drew her irresistibly towards him, the craving stronger than anger or fear. 'You can insult me, hurt me, hate me... test me any way you like. I'm strong. I'm not going to run away just because things aren't perfect between us...'

Somehow her hands were on his chest and she was bending over him, touching her mouth to his, even as she protested in a sighing whisper, 'This has to be the last time, Scott...'

He laughed and suddenly she was beneath him instead of on top of him and this time there was no trembling hesitation or clumsy eagerness in his movements; he was all sensual male dominance, supremely confident of his appeal, daring her to deny the evidence of her own passion as he danced her with him from peak to breathless peak.

'The last time? Never!' he growled as she shattered in his arms, pouring his dauntless certainty into her mind as he poured the essence of his maleness deep into her welcoming body. 'This is a beginning for us, Grace, not an end. You can't stop this happening any more than you can stop the sun shining or the rain falling. This is *our* time. You love me, Grace, I can feel it in every breath and sigh and bitter word...'

Perhaps she *couldn't* stop herself loving him, but she could at least try one last gamble:

'All right——'

'All right what?' His slick, hot body was still moving against her in lazy undulations.

'You win.'

He stilled and lifted his head, alert to the strained nuance in her voice. 'And what precisely do I win, Grace?' he murmured.

'Blair Components. Me.' The order of her words was achingly deliberate. She dragged up the sheet and held it across her bare body as he jackknifed into sitting position beside her.

'What do you mean, Blair Components?' he asked harshly.

'You need it under your control, don't you—to squeeze RedWing even further out on a limb so that you can complete your cycle of revenge? Well, it's yours. A gift. No strings.'

The black eyes were unfathomable, deep, dark pools filled with cold, murky currents. Grace swallowed, waiting tensely. Was he going to fling her sacrifice back in her face? Tell her that he was insulted? That his love was unconditional, untainted by past bitterness or present ambition? Oh, please, please...

'Thank you.' He said it quietly, politely, and Grace felt something inside her die.

'I...I'd prefer it if you kept the name Blair,' she said numbly, forcing herself to be practical, unable to quite believe that she had burnt her bridges so thoroughly. 'And...I—I'd like to continue working there——'

'No strings, you said.' He was out of the bed, dressing as swiftly as he had disrobed, but calmly, emotionlessly, suddenly as sober as a judge.

Grace stared at him, her subconscious hopes revealed for the wishful fantasies that they were. Now, at least, she knew exactly where she stood. She had offered and he had accepted. This was the reality she had needed to face. Scott was a businessman first and foremost, and always would be. She knew it would be the height of insanity to enter into a relationship with him believing that she could change him. She also knew that love was the mistress of pride. She would have him, and pay the price, if not eagerly, then at least willingly.

'It'll take a couple of days to have a legal transfer drawn up. Will you do it, or shall I?'

He had everything else; she might as well give him this, too.

'You do it.'

'Very well. And, Grace...?' She paused in the act of picking up her scattered clothes, her pale nudity cloaked in a mantle of quiet dignity. His expression was implacably cool. She lifted her chin in unconscious defiance of the apprehension that feathered down her spine.

His voice matched his inflexible expression. 'The second clause of your generous offer is also non-negotiable.

'You move in with me tomorrow.'

CHAPTER ELEVEN

THE deed of transfer was signed three days later in the stylish penthouse boardroom of Scott Electronics, witnessed by a shell-shocked Neville and an unreasonably amused Mike Patrick.

It was only when Scott's corporation lawyer produced a second agreement that Grace realised the reason for his inappropriate manner.

'What is this?' she snapped. Was Scott now asking her to sign away her soul, as well as her pride and her independent livelihood?

'Just a formality,' Scott drawled soothingly, from miles away across the polished table. He had treated her with just such gentle indulgence ever since she had meekly folded to his dominating hand. 'But by all means read it through to make sure that I'm not taking unfair advantage of you.'

It only took a few moments. It was very simple, very straightforward and *very* compromising. Couched in starkly unlegal terms, it was a confession, a fantasy, a poem . . .

It was a marriage contract and it contained a bride-price. Fifty per cent of Scott Electronics.

The silver pen dropped out of Grace's nerveless hands and rolled noisily across the polished table towards the enigmatic man facing her.

Scott leaned forward and slowly picked it up. Not taking his eyes off her flushed face, he stood and walked around the table, holding out the elegantly engraved cylinder.

'Aren't the terms favourable enough, Grace? Do you want more? Sixty per cent? A hundred? Give me a figure.' He leant over her shoulder to strike out the offending clause and Grace pushed the pen away, hugging the paper to her tumultuous breast.

'What's going on? What's he demanding now? Grace, why are you looking like that?' She was fuzzily aware of Neville's blustering outrage receding as Mike Patrick shepherded him out of the room with a low-voiced explanation.

She needed a few explanations herself. 'This is a very bad joke...' she choked, and the bent head close to hers turned, only a kiss away.

'No joke, Grace. Trust has to start somewhere—if not with you then with me. Marriage is a partnership. Fifty-fifty seemed a good place to start.'

She tried, very hard, to find some sustaining outrage. 'You put me through hell! You let me think that I was less important than your damned revenge. And you never even *mentioned* marriage!'

'You didn't give me the chance,' he pointed out drily. 'You were too busy putting my integrity to the test yet again, dangling the luscious bait under my nose, waiting for me to reveal my true colours so that you could decide whether I was worthy of your love. You made me very, *very* angry, Grace...'

'I wasn't trying to——' He lifted her chin, her guilty eyes met his and she saw the stark pain that he had concealed under the arrogant calm of the last few days and was lost...

'I thought that was what you wanted,' she whispered weakly. 'I wasn't going to let it matter to us...'

'No, I realised that just in time to pull me back from the brink of a very nasty tantrum. But I was certainly angry enough to want to punish you for your faithlessness. So I took what I didn't want in order to teach you not to make reckless assumptions in future. And now it's time for you to take *your* medicine...' He took the now crumpled paper from her nerveless fingers and smoothed it out in front of her. 'Sign. I won't marry you, Grace, until you agree that we share... *everything*. The good as well as the bad.'

She couldn't believe this was the same ruthless tycoon who had asset-stripped his way to success. 'But... you weren't serious. I won't let you. You—this must be worth millions.'

He told her exactly how many. And still held out the pen.

'Is it legal?'

'As hell! Mike is hoping it's just a grand gesture that you will lovingly decline. He doesn't know it's not an option.'

His grim amusement convinced her. 'I don't want your money, Scott. I just want you.' She wasn't aware of the tears jewelling her eyes.

'Too bad.' He lifted her hand and wrapped her pale fingers around the pen.

'What about RedWing... your revenge?' she husked, looking at him, rather than at the declaration of love that he was tracing her shaky signature across.

'Revenge? That was just a substitute for what was really missing from my life. My best revenge will to be live well with the woman I love. I have more lofty goals to aim for now. The baby I promised to give you, for one.' He made a throaty sound of deep satisfaction as he folded the paper and tucked it securely in the inside pocket of his jacket. 'Now there's no way you can back out. If you ever try to leave me we'll be tied up in the courts together for decades, trying to sort out the legal tangle. Come on. We have places to go, things to do.'

He helped her on with her coat and led her to the door.

'Where are we going?' asked Grace meekly. It wouldn't have surprised her if Scott had a justice of the peace stashed in his office downstairs.

He slanted her a smile that curled her toes. 'I think it's about time you conquered that problem you seem to have with lifts. Perhaps you need a very powerful positive experience to replace the negative memory.'

'The *lift*?'

He shared her startled laughter. 'Don't worry, it's a private one,' he teased. 'It would be awfully appropriate, don't you think, Grace, if our first child was conceived in a lift?'

Grace's skin began to tingle with warmth as he loosened his tie and lazily keyed the control outside the unmarked lift. Dark sultry eyes smouldered over her coat.

'It's not fur, but it'll have to do. Button it up, there's a darling. We have to get this re-enactment as accurate as possible...'

And, with a lot of wicked laughter and a great deal of love, they did...

WORDFIND #5

```
A U C K L A N D J E V D S B
F A Z Q W N M E O L K F A S
V B S E C R E T H X C T B C
J T U I O P L E P I T J L W
N Z A X C R T R N L Y T O I
E D F E L P O M E J H G U D
W E R C F D X I R O I M N O
Z Y J A K L P N A P I E R W
E R E R I M D A H G D S Q X
A C B G N M L T P O Y U Y T
L Q A Z X S T I W E D C V F
A I T I U O R O M A N C E T
N Y H N C U K N L O I D W V
D U K S Y R O G E R G J B X
```

ADMIRER	NAPIER
AUCKLAND	NEW ZEALAND
BATTLE	ROMANCE
DETERMINATION	SCOTT
GRACE	SECRET
GREGORY	WIDOW

**Look for A YEAR DOWN UNDER Wordfind #6
in June's Harlequin Presents #1562
OUTBACK MAN by Miranda Lee.**   WF5

HARLEQUIN PRESENTS®

A Year
DOWN UNDER

In 1993, Harlequin Presents celebrates the land down
under. In June, let us take you to the Australian Outback,
in OUTBACK MAN by Miranda Lee,
Harlequin Presents #1562.

Surviving a plane crash in the Australian Outback is
surely enough trauma to endure. So why does Adrianna
have to be rescued by Bryce McLean, a man so gorgeous
that he turns all her cherished beliefs upside-down? But
the desert proves to be an intimate and seductive setting
and suddenly Adrianna's only realities are the red-hot
dust *and* Bryce....

Share the adventure—and the romance—
of A Year Down Under!

SOLUTIONS TO
WORDFIND #5

A	U	C	K	L	A	N	D	J	E	V	D	S	B
F	A	Z	Q	W	N	M	E	O	L	K	F	A	S
V	B	S	E	C	R	E	T	H	X	C	T	B	C
J	T	U	I	O	P	L	E	P	I	T	J	L	W
N	Z	A	X	C	R	T	R	N	L	Y	T	O	I
E	D	F	E	L	P	O	M	E	J	H	G	U	D
W	E	R	C	F	D	X	I	R	O	I	M	N	O
Z	Y	J	A	K	L	P	N	A	P	I	E	R	W
Z	A	R	E	R	I	M	D	A	H	G	D	S	Q	X
E	C	B	G	N	M	L	T	P	O	Y	U	Y	T
A	Q	I	A	Z	X	S	T	I	W	E	D	C	V	F
L	A	T	I	U	O	R	O	M	A	N	C	E	T
A	N	Y	H	N	C	U	K	N	L	O	I	D	W	V
D	U	K	S	V	R	O	G	E	R	G	J	B	X

YDU-MYA